Silent
Dreams

SUSAN K. DRONEY

This is a work of fiction. Names, characters, places, and incidents are products of the author's imagination or are used fictitiously and are not to be construed as real. Any resemblance to actual events, locations, organizations, or persons, living or dead, is entirely coincidental.

World Castle Publishing, LLC
Pensacola, Florida
Copyright © Susan K. Droney 2017
Paperback ISBN: 9781629896090
eBook ISBN: 9781629896106
First Edition World Castle Publishing, LLC, January 23, 2017
http://www.worldcastlepublishing.com

Licensing Notes

Cover: Karen Fuller
Editor: Lisa Petrocelli

Chapter One

Kami Matthews gazed out of the grimy window and watched the day slowly fade into dusk. She sighed heavily as she turned her pretty blonde head away from the window and glanced at the clock on the stained wall. "Wow!" she exclaimed. "I didn't realize it was so late! I've got to get out of here." She gave her friend a quick hug. "Don't worry," she said brightly. "Everything will work out. You'll see. Be thankful that nothing worse happened."

"I guess so," Blaine Kirsten mumbled, staring down at her faded jeans. "I wish you could stay a little longer though." She looked up hopefully at Kami. "Please?" she pleaded. "I...I don't want to be alone. I'm scared, Kami. Please stay for just another hour."

Kami's eyes clouded. "I'm sorry, Blaine, but I really do have to go. I'll see you tomorrow, I promise," she said, moving to the door. She laid her hand on the doorknob, and then turned to her friend. "It'll be all right. You worry too much." She patted Blaine's shoulder. "Try to get some rest now and things won't look so bad tomorrow."

"I hope," Blaine slowly answered as Kami opened the door. "But I doubt it. I don't think I'll ever be the same." She quietly shut the door behind Kami.

Kami slipped into the darkened hallway and leaned against the closed door for a few seconds debating whether she should go back inside to comfort Blaine. She couldn't stand leaving her in the emotional state she was in, but she needed to get home. She'd already been gone longer than she should have. She carefully made her way down the litter-strewn stench-filled hallway and hurried outside, anxious to get some fresh air into her burning nostrils. She jumped into her yellow sports car and sped through the run-down neighborhood, eager to reach her own safe and familiar surroundings. She parked her car in the parking garage and quickly walked to her building.

"Good evening, Miss Matthews," a man warmly greeted her as he held the door.

She nodded. "Good evening. Are there any messages for me, John?" She fumbled in her purse for her apartment key.

"Yes." John's thin lips immediately turned into a frown. "Mr. Barnes rang me several times when you didn't answer your cell phone. He insists that you return his call upon your arrival."

Kami frowned as she looked at the middle-aged man. He was thin, single, and lived in a small apartment in the basement. "I will."

He peered at her through thick glasses. "He is in a nasty mood," he gently warned. "I convinced him that it wasn't necessary for him to come over. He'd thought maybe you'd had an accident so I checked your apartment to make sure you hadn't. I told him you probably were held up in traffic."

"Thank you, John," Kami said. She sighed tiredly as he held the elevator door for her.

She knew that John would have received the brunt of

Josh's foul mood if he had come over. But, as in the past, John hopefully stalled Josh with a believable excuse for her lateness. She liked John, but she'd never understand how Josh's money could persuade him to take this type of position. She wasn't sure what his title was. What she did know was that he was actually a spy for Josh. He reported the comings and goings and who came in or out of every apartment. She wondered when he slept, as he always appeared whenever the main door was opened. She assumed that something was rigged up in his apartment to alert him. As she became acquainted with the man, she'd gained his trust and respect, and at the same time some of her freedom. He'd looked the other way many times and Josh was never the wiser for it. The loss of her freedom was what she missed the most. She'd give up all of the money and luxuries if she could regain her freedom. But she knew that was a futile wish. She'd sold her soul to the devil.

"Good night, John." She pressed a few bills into his palm.

"Good night, Miss Matthews." He pushed her floor button, and then released the door.

Once inside her apartment, Kami flicked on the lamps in the entrance hall and the living room, then sank wearily into a chair as she grabbed her cell phone. She dreaded making the call and waited a couple of minutes before pressing his number. Maybe he won't answer, she thought. Sometimes he didn't when he was out tracking down one of his other girls. She needed time to gather her thoughts, but unfortunately, he answered on the first ring. She braced herself for his angry tirade which she knew would be forthcoming. Every time she angered him, he became more violent.

"Hello, Josh. This is Kami," she said in a low but soft voice.

"Where the hell have you been? I've been trying to reach

5

you for hours! You'd better have a damned good explanation!" he stormed.

"I was with Blaine. Where else would I be?" she innocently answered.

"Why didn't you answer your cell phone?"

"I turned it off because I needed to talk uninterrupted to her."

"You know that your phone is to be on at all times. I need to be able to reach you at a moment's notice!" he shouted. "And?" he demanded.

"And what?"

"Don't play games with me, Kami. If you value your life, you'll cut the act!"

She chewed her bottom lip. "I couldn't do it, Josh. It wasn't the right time. You should've seen her. Some creep roughed her up and almost raped her last night. She's in bad shape."

"You have twenty-four hours to talk to Blaine and convince her to work for me—no more, no less. Do I make myself clear?"

"Josh, there's no way Blaine will go for it. She's different— you know what I mean—too innocent. I can't force her to do this. All the other girls came on board willingly. I'm sure there are a lot of girls who would love to join, but not Blaine. I think this is a bad business decision."

"How I run the business is no concern of yours."

"But Josh, what you're asking me to do is illegal."

"Twenty-four hours!" he snarled. "Don't cross me, Kami."

The line went dead. "Dammit! Now what do I do?" she muttered to herself as she leaned back in her chair and squeezed her eyes shut. Her head pounded near her temples. She prepared herself for another in a series of what were rapidly becoming daily headaches. How had she allowed herself to get into this mess? But more importantly, how could she keep Blaine out of it? She needed time, but time was the one thing that Josh Barnes would never give her. Patience was not one of his virtues. In fact, when it came right down to it, it appeared he had no worthy virtues to speak of. He lived for money. How to get more was his top priority, and God help the person who stood in his way. When he demanded something, he expected immediate results and she knew from experience how severe the consequences could be if his orders were not obeyed.

****

Blaine locked her apartment door and slid a straight-backed chair under the doorknob. She sat on her worn sofa drawing her knees to her chin. She was grateful that Kami had spent the entire day consoling her. It was selfish of her to expect Kami to stay any longer. After all, Kami had taken the day off from work and had canceled her after-work activities to comfort her in her time of need. Kami was the only person Blaine felt comfortable enough with to share all of her problems. And lately she seemed to have many. Luck had never been on her side and she doubted it ever would be. She lived life one day at a time, long ago having given up hope for anything better.

Blaine had always been a loner, never quite feeling that she fit in anywhere. At the age of twenty-two she was jaded and surmised that her cynical outlook on life most likely stemmed from the loss of her natural parents when she was just an infant. She'd been adopted and raised by a loving couple, but a part of her felt disconnected from the Kirstens. Their family history wasn't hers, even though they loved and treated her as their biological child. She longed to know all the things that made her who *she* was. She wanted to know what her birth parents had looked like and what their lives had been like. What hopes and dreams had they held? Had they been happy and contented and deeply in love? Had she been wanted? Did she have any brothers and sisters? All the unanswered questions haunted her dreams as she prayed for some way to remember the first few months of her life. What would her life have been like if they'd lived? How different would her life be today?

****

Detectives Casey Jorgan and Jane Adams sat across from one another at their adjoining desks, using their lunch hour to review cases between bites of food.

Casey picked up a napkin and dabbed at her mouth. "I think we can wrap up this Booker case," she stated confidently.

Jane's eyebrows shot up. "I'd like to know how. We're no closer now than when we started." She cocked an eyebrow at her eager colleague. "Unless you know something I don't?"

"I have a plan," Casey said, stretching. "If I wouldn't be imposing, I'd like to come over to your apartment tonight and fill you in. I'll even bring a bottle of wine." She grinned widely.

Jane made a face at her. "I don't like the sound of that, Casey. The last time you came over with a bottle of wine, we ended up staying awake the whole night going over theories." She rolled her eyes. "As I recall, some of your theories when you're filled with wine are the stuff Hollywood movies are made of."

Casey laughed. "Not this time. I promise." She held up her hand. "Scout's Honor."

"Since when were you ever a scout?"

"I could have been." She took another bite of her sandwich. "Guess who's coming?"

Before Jane could respond, Lieutenant Richardson, smiling broadly, walked over to their desks. "I'm pleased to see my two favorite detectives enjoying their work."

Casey cocked a suspicious eye. "I don't think I like the sound of that, Lt. Richardson. Besides, it's our lunch hour." She winked at Jane with a mischievous twinkle in her eyes.

He checked his wristwatch. "Late lunch hour," he observed.

"We were running leads all day," Jane explained. "This was the first chance we've had to grab a bite, but we're going over our cases while we eat."

The balding, thin man leaned over Casey's desk. "I think that you two will be perfect for this case. She gave a statement, but refuses to come down to the station to identify possible suspects. See if you can convince her. Go over the file tonight and go see her tomorrow morning." He threw a file on her desk. "Enjoy your lunch."

Jane nodded as she pulled her chair over to Casey's desk. She picked up the clean manila folder knowing that in a couple of days it would be worn and grimy due to the handling it would inevitably receive.

"What is it? Another drug case?" Casey asked, finishing her lunch.

"Blaine Kirsten," Jane slowly read flipping through the file. "Looks like an assault and attempted rape."

"What was the name?" The color drained from Casey's cheeks.

Jane looked quizzically at her. "What's wrong?" she asked. "Do you know her or something?"

Casey drew a deep breath. "No," she quickly answered as she reached for the folder with trembling hands.

****

Blaine took a long, hot bath, then climbed into bed with a romance novel, hoping to escape the terror of the previous night for a little while. She opened the book, but her mind refused to concentrate on the words, instead it took her back to that terrifying moment she was attacked. She'd tried to fight back, but he'd overpowered her, punched, and kicked her. She could still feel his putrid breath as his large damp hands clawed at her flesh ripping her clothes from her body. She shuddered. Thank God for the passerby who had come to her rescue when she screamed. God only knows what might have happened to her if he hadn't shown up at that precise moment. She would have been raped and possibly murdered. She would have become just another statistic on the police blotter in a city that was overrun with crime.

Having her life hanging in the balance, not knowing whether she would live or die, brought out a new fear in her. Her destiny had been in that bastard's hands. He'd taken control and had left her powerless at that moment. She'd never forget how cold and clammy her skin felt with every touch from him. Her feeling of helplessness had choked her with fear, but the anonymous passerby had changed her destiny and she hadn't even gotten his name. He'd disappeared as soon as the police arrived.

After the police had relentlessly questioned her about every tiny detail, she came back to her small apartment where she sat trembling in a chair all night until the first rays of sunlight filtered through her windows. That was when she called Kami. She couldn't stand her aloneness anymore.

A tear slid from her eye. She knew that her adopted parents had wanted a good and happy life for her, but how would they feel if they knew how she was living today? When they'd died, shortly after her high school graduation, she found herself all alone in the world. Every day the loneliness suffocated her a little more. She desperately ached to be part of a family. She wanted to belong somewhere. But she had no one. The Kirstens had had no other children and she'd never met their distant relatives. The only way she'd have the roots and family she desperately craved was if she met the perfect man…a man who would love her and fill the empty void in her life and give her a houseful of children. So far, that perfect man had eluded her, and all she could do was struggle to survive with the empty hollowness inside her heart.

****

Kami climbed into her king-sized bed and pulled her comforter to her chin. She put her hands beneath her head and stared up at the ceiling. She needed to come up with a plan, but had no clue where to begin. Time definitely was not on her side. Josh had made that perfectly clear. She chewed her bottom lip. She had to be cautious with Blaine, enticing her without letting her know it was a trap. Josh wouldn't be put off any longer. If only she could think of something, anything, to stall him for just a little longer. She removed her hands and rolled onto her side. She stroked the silk sheet. Her apartment was lavish compared to the rattrap Blaine called home, but if she made one wrong move, she'd be back in the gutter and all of this would be gone in a flash. She blew her breath out. If only Blaine was someone she didn't care about it would be so much easier. But she *did* care about her. Blaine was not only her friend, but Blaine trusted her. Kami loved Blaine like a sister and treasured their friendship, but how would Blaine feel about her when she learned the truth? More importantly, Kami wondered how she would ever be able to live with herself after she betrayed Blaine in the worst imaginable way. Her lips trembled as tears stung her eyes.

Her breathing became raspy as the threatened tears brimmed, and then fell from her eyes.

****

Josh Barnes sat at his desk poring over the receipts from the past week. He was pleased with the results, but still it wasn't enough. It would never be enough. He stretched his tall muscular frame, and then focused on the neat columns of figures. His insatiable appetite for money and sex was what had led him to this lucrative business years ago. He smiled knowing only too well the price a man would pay for a good fuck. His business wasn't founded on the cheap street-walking prostitutes any idiot could buy for a few bucks, but a business with a bevy of the most beautiful, intelligent, and sophisticated women he could find. He prided himself on his girls' immaculate hygiene and grooming. After a thorough medical and dental examination, and a drug screening, only the best were employed. Every inch of their bodies was checked and whatever cosmetic surgery Josh deemed necessary to further enhance their appearances, the women had willingly done at his expense. He spent a fortune on clothing and extravagant apartments. He owned them and that was a fact they had to live with in exchange for wealth and comfort beyond their wildest dreams. They sold their bodies to him to use for any purpose that suited him.

He never had a problem recruiting new girls. Their eyes would light up at the mention of money beyond their wildest dreams. He used his natural charm to convince a young beauty that caught his eye to become a part of his exclusive organization. Most of the women fell for him, and of course he let them believe they were exclusive to him and him only. Only after he caught them in his net, they learned the truth. Once in, never out. Anyone who was foolish enough to betray him soon regretted the decision. His girls knew the consequences if they ever tried to deceive him, and the few that had tried regretted their actions.

He was a self-made millionaire and he'd be damned if anyone would take his empire away from him. He'd worked too long and too hard to get where he was. He didn't fear legal repercussions smug in the knowledge that a vast majority of dignitaries were his best clients. He was as cold as he was passionate. There was no middle ground and that was the way he intended to keep it. He despised weaklings and learned long ago that to make it in the world one had to throw away the preconceived ideas of morality and go after what one wanted at any cost. Otherwise, someone else would come along and grab it.

Blaine Kirsten was different from any woman he'd ever met though. Her innocence and overt beauty had captivated him from the moment he first laid eyes on her. He wanted her no matter what it took, and when he wanted something, it was only a matter of time before he got it. Anything or anybody could be bought for the right price. He smiled smugly. Kami would come through for him. She always did. She had no choice. Blaine would soon be his. He could barely hold his emotions in check as he imagined how it was going to feel to hold her delicate body in his strong arms. Yes, soon she would be his. He had big plans for her.

Chapter Two

Kami looked sympathetically at Blaine. Her gracefully chiseled features, smoky gray deep-set eyes, and long auburn hair cascaded over her slender shoulders alluding to an almost childlike innocence. Blaine Kirsten possessed an alluring beauty, and many times Kami wondered if Blaine even realized how truly beautiful she was. If she did, she never acted like it or used it to her advantage. She did know that Blaine's naivety, shyness, and lack of self-esteem could never endure what Josh Barnes would demand of her.

Kami's stomach muscles tightened. She swallowed hard, fighting the urge, and then drew a deep breath. "How are you feeling today?" she asked softly. "Better, I hope."

Blaine's forehead creased. "I'm scared, Kami." Her lips trembled as she spoke. "I got a call from the cops. I guess they caught the creep who attacked me." She sighed. "A couple of detectives are coming over in a few minutes. A teenager was attacked last night near where I was attacked. I saw it on the news. She was beaten and raped."

"That's terrible, Blaine!" Kami cried as she grabbed Blaine's hand. She would give anything to erase the haunting fear she saw in Blaine's eyes.

Blaine shuddered. "He took my purse with my ID in it.

14

He could come here at any time!"

Kami frowned. "I thought you just said they caught him."

"I'm still scared." She rubbed her temples. "Why is this happening to me?" Her eyes brimmed with tears. "What did I do to deserve this?"

Kami saw the faint shadows under Blaine's eyes. "Stay with me," she quickly offered. "You know how large my place is. I have more than enough room. We'd have fun. Come on," she urged. "You need to relax and get away from here, just until this is over."

Blaine shrugged. "I don't know. I'll see." She took another sip of coffee. "I can't think straight right now."

A soft knock sounded on the door. Blaine set her cup down. "Who's there?" she anxiously called. She stood and cautiously walked toward the door.

"Detective Jorgan."

Blaine removed the lock and slowly opened the door leaving the security chain on. "I thought two of you were coming," she said suspiciously.

"It's just me for now," Casey said as she tried to get a look at the young woman through the partially opened door. "May I come in?" she asked, holding her shield in front of Blaine.

"I'm sorry," Blaine replied as she removed the chain, then flung the door wide open. "I've been so nervous. Sure, come on in," she stuttered.

Casey's breath caught in her throat as she viewed Blaine up close. She cleared her throat, composing herself. "That's understandable," she answered as her eyes scrutinized the small rundown flat, and then came to rest once again on the frightened young woman's face.

"This is my friend Kami Matthews," Blaine said

motioning with a slight wave of a hand in Kami's direction.

Casey nodded at Kami, who stood silently not acknowledging the detective.

"Please sit down," Blaine offered. "Can I get you anything? Coffee...tea?"

"No, thank you," Casey politely declined as she seated herself on the worn sofa. She pulled a notepad and pen from her pocket. "Blaine, tell me everything you can remember about the attack."

Blaine sighed heavily. "I already told the police everything I know." She looked evenly at Casey.

"I know you did, but now I want you to tell me. Maybe you'll remember something else. I'll be handling your case along with Detective Adams."

Blaine wrung her hands and began pacing back and forth across the threadbare brown stained living room carpet. "He was a big guy...at least six feet and he was stocky."

"Were there any distinguishing marks? A scar or tattoo?"

She shook her head. "I don't know. It was dark." She stopped pacing and sank into a chair. "I thought the girl he attacked last night gave a description of him. I was told he was caught."

"I don't believe you were told by the police department that the man who attacked *you* was caught. You must have misunderstood. There is no way we can be certain that the two attacks are related unless a positive ID is made."

Blaine frowned but kept silent.

Casey's heart went out to Blaine. It was obvious from looking around the shabby room that Blaine Kirsten was desperately trying to survive in a world that from the looks of it had only dealt her one cruel blow after another. She'd seen it repeatedly in the hollow eyes of victim after victim.

Now Blaine was one of those victims and it pissed Casey off. Jane and she had been going over the file last night when they were notified of the attack on the teenager. It fit the same MO, but it could still be two isolated attacks. If Blaine refused to make a positive identification, the scumbag who attacked her could still be roaming the streets searching for his next victim. Whoever had attacked Blaine was violent and needed to be taken off the streets as soon as possible.

"I want to help you, Blaine," Casey said gently. "I want to put the monster away who attacked you." She hoped to gain Blaine's trust. Once she gained a victim's trust, the rest of her job came easier.

"Detective, I'm trying to convince Blaine to stay at my place with me for a while," Kami broke in. "She's terrified staying here."

Casey eyed Blaine. "That might be a good idea," she said without taking her eyes off Blaine. "Blaine, try to remember everything you can. Where were you going when you were attacked?"

Blaine bit her bottom lip. "I was coming home from work. I work at Sischo's Department Store. I work the late shift and get off at ten."

"Did you take the bus home?"

She nodded. "I always do to and from. The last stop is two blocks from here. I've walked this same route for the past year without anyone ever bothering me at night. I've always felt safe here. There are decent people in the neighborhood and we always look out for one another."

Casey's eyes narrowed. "It's not safe for a young woman to be walking alone after dark anywhere."

Blaine's lips drew into a firm narrow line. "My personal driver wasn't available to pick me up," she replied sarcastically.

Casey ignored her sarcasm. "What else do you recall about your attacker? Did he say anything to you? Would you recognize his voice if you heard it again?"

Blaine blew her breath out in a rush. "There's nothing more to tell." Her lips quivered. "I'm so sick and tired of all these questions! That monster's got my ID. He knows where I live. He could come busting in here anytime he feels like it! You should be out there hunting him down instead of asking me the same questions over and over. I'm the victim, remember? Or have you forgotten?"

Kami's eyebrows knitted together. "I'm confused. I thought you said he was picked up after attacking that teenager, Blaine. So he's not the same guy?"

Blaine twisted her hands together. "I assumed he was since I got a call from the police saying the description I gave matched the asshole they picked up."

"So no one from the department told you that it was the same man who'd attacked you. You went on your own assumptions." Casey peered at her. "Just because your physical description matched doesn't mean it's the same perp," she explained. "That's why I need your cooperation," she gently urged as she continued to study Blaine. "Were you sexually assaulted in any way? On your report you stated that you weren't penetrated, but did he make any other sexual contact?"

Blaine covered her face with her hands. "No," she softly sobbed. "But he would've if someone hadn't come by. That person saved my life and I don't even know his name." Tears ran from her eyes and streamed down her pale cheeks. "I don't know any more. I told you I already gave the report down at the station. You can read that. There's nothing else I remember to add to it."

Casey frowned. She hated forcing victims to relive the horror they'd just been through, but it was the only way to find a piece of information that maybe had inadvertently been omitted in prior statements. She'd seen it happen too many times before. "Did you seek medical attention after you reported the attack?"

"No. My bruises will fade." Blaine brushed the tears from her cheeks.

"You might have some internal injuries. You should get checked out."

"I'll be fine," Blaine said heatedly.

"Why are you *really* refusing to come down to the station?" Casey asked pointedly near the point of exasperation. "What are you afraid of?"

She blinked rapidly and swallowed hard. "Let the other victim identify him."

Casey gritted her teeth. It was hard to maintain her cool. She silently counted to ten. How could she get through to her? "What are you not getting, Blaine? He may not be the same man who attacked you. Help us put away whoever did this to you."

"He could be."

"Blaine, you're not making any sense," Kami said. "One minute you're afraid he'll come here since he has your ID, and the next you assume he's been picked up. You need to find out one way or the other." She frowned. "If you don't, you'll never have peace. You'll always be looking over your shoulder."

Blaine ran a trembling hand through her hair. "I just want this over. I want things to go back to normal."

"Unless you come down to the station to look at a lineup,

nothing will be normal. You'll always wonder if we got your attacker, too, or if he's still lurking out there somewhere. You'll never know where he is or when he'll show up." Casey stood, frustrated that she was getting nowhere with the woman. The fear was in Blaine's eyes, but whatever was going on in her mind was beyond Casey's comprehension. There was nothing more she could say. "Stay with your friend," she advised as she put her pen and notepad in her pocket. "I'll keep in touch with you."

"Sure you will," Blaine replied. "I'll bet you have more important cases to work on. Put this on the back burner until the scumbag commits murder the next time!"

"What do you expect me to do?" Casey was rapidly losing her patience. "I can't do anything without your cooperation." Her eyes narrowed as she looked at the younger woman. "You need to come down to the station or my hands are tied."

Blaine emphatically shook her head. Her eyes flared. "I said no."

Casey's jaw tightened. "You may not believe this, but I'm on your side, Blaine. This isn't going on the back burner — none of my cases do. I'll do everything in my power to try to find and put him away for good, but it's going to be difficult without your help." She looked at Kami. "Miss Matthews, try to convince her to stay with you for a while." She took her notepad and pen back out of her pocket and handed them to Kami. "Please write down your address and phone number in case I need to contact you."

"Of course." Kami scribbled the information on the notepad. "I'll take care of her, Detective Jorgan. I promise."

"I'll bet the guy that was picked up is the same guy who attacked me," Blaine said.

Casey's jaw tightened. Was she serious? Hadn't she heard a word that had been said? She wished she could shake some sense into her. "Maybe…maybe not. The description you gave could match a hundred suspects. We can't charge him with your attack unless you make a positive identification."

Blaine tensed. "So you may or may not have caught the creep who attacked me. Is that what you're telling me?"

Casey hoped Blaine was finally relenting. She needed to get the woman down to the station. "Yes, Blaine. That is what I've been trying to explain to you. We could be looking at two different men in unrelated cases." She peered at her. "I can drive you to the station and when you're finished bring you back here or to Miss Matthews' residence if you prefer."

She was silent for a minute. Her forehead creased as she peered at Casey. "No," she said firmly. "I…I don't want to look at him again." She shivered.

Casey seethed inside. "I can't force you." She turned to Kami. "Maybe you can convince her." She turned her attention back to Blaine. "I think you should stay with your friend."

Blaine's jaw tightened. "What choice do I have?"

****

Casey drove cautiously through the noon hour traffic. Blaine Kirsten firmly cemented herself in her thoughts. She hated this kind of case. It was exasperating and even though she couldn't let Blaine know, the bastard, if he was indeed the one who'd attacked Blaine, probably would be back on the streets before the ink was even dry on his arrest warrant. The courts and prisons were already too overcrowded to give top priority over an assault. She loved her job, but at times found it difficult to separate her own emotions from the task. And this case certainly grated on her emotions. Emotions that she had to keep bottled up inside. At least for now. If she

21

didn't keep a handle on her emotions, she could jeopardize everything. Blaine couldn't know the reason Casey felt like a bottle ready to pop its cork. She couldn't know that Casey desperately wanted to help her. In time she would learn the truth, but now wasn't the right time. And Casey didn't know when the right time would ever be. There was too much at stake...for the both of them.

Casey's eyebrows drew together. Blaine was exactly as Casey always imagined she would be—a beautiful young woman. But she'd thought Blaine's life would have turned out much better—at least that's what she'd hoped. Still, even though life hadn't treated Blaine kindly, the future could be brighter and if Casey had anything to say about it, it definitely would be. Casey needed to tread lightly with Blaine.

Casey turned on the radio and after several unsuccessful attempts to locate a station that suited her, she turned it off. She weaved in and out of traffic, her mind soon drifting to her own past. She didn't put the entire blame on her ex-husband Mark for the dissolution of their marriage after only five years, as most of her friends did. She was as much to blame as he was. Mark had wanted children, but Casey had kept putting him off, insisting that she needed to get her career established first. She'd always dreamed of being a detective and watched every TV show and cop movie she could find, mesmerizing herself in the action and cheering when the bad guy received his just reward at the hands of an honest and uncorrupted cop. Her friends silently sat by, amused with her and what they perceived at the time to be just a passing fancy, but it didn't pass. It only grew deeper, with her aspiration of being a detective intensifying during her teenage years until it consumed most of her waking as well as sleeping hours.

Casey would allow nothing to come between her and

her dream, not even her husband, even though he always appeared to support her in her quest and spent countless hours helping her study and then drilling her for the detective's exam. In the end, though, she found that he hadn't supported her at all, only pretended to. It hurt. By the time she made detective, Mark informed her that he had found someone who wanted the same things he did. She didn't fight to keep him. The divorce was quick and simple. A month later, he had remarried. To hide her pain Casey threw herself even more intensely into her work. From then on, she devoted her life only to her career and the quest to find out what had happened to her only blood relative — her sister.

She pulled up in front of the precinct, got out of the car, and hurried inside. "How's Stan?"

Jane laughed. "Just a bump on the head, but from the way he was carrying on, you'd think he'd been knocked unconscious."

Casey smiled. "I'm glad he wasn't seriously injured."

"Me, too," she replied relief evident in her voice. "Did you get Blaine Kirsten to ID the perp?"

"No." Casey sat down at her desk and absentmindedly shuffled through some papers. "She refuses."

"Did she remember anything else about the attack?"

"No," Casey replied as she raised her eyes. "Maybe you should talk to her, Jane."

Jane frowned. "Why? If she won't cooperate with you, I doubt she will with me. Did you tell her we can't do anything unless she comes down here?"

"I did, but she won't budge." She rubbed her temples. "We've got to convince her somehow, Jane."

"Why? If she refuses, then there's nothing we can do. The case will go cold. Come on, Casey. We can't force her.

You know that." Jane peered at her. "Why the long face?" She leaned in closer. "It's not just this case, is it? What's really going on with you? And don't say nothing because I know you better than that."

She frowned. "I don't know." She flashed a tight smile. "Maybe it's the big three-oh facing me in a few weeks. I'm dreading that one."

Jane laughed. "It's not that bad. Remember I went through it a couple of years ago."

Casey grinned. "How could I forget? You had the whole precinct feeling sorry for you. You acted like your life was over and that it was the end of the world. I don't know how Stan put up with it."

"I don't either," she admitted, "but I got through it. So, cheer up! You know the saying...you're not getting older, you're getting better."

Casey grimaced. "I suppose, but I really hate that expression." She leaned her elbows on her desk. "Sometimes I feel like time is slipping away. Every year seems to get shorter. One day I'll wake up, be sixty, and wonder where the time went."

Jane stared thoughtfully at her. "Maybe you need a vacation, Casey. You rarely take time off. Go somewhere exotic and lie on the beach all day. Forget about everything else. It'll do you a world of good."

"And I'd go stir crazy the first day." She grinned. "So did you come up with anything new on the Booker case?"

Jane's eyes darkened. "A dead end." She sighed heavily. "We're banging our heads against a wall on this one. There are too many drug dealers out there, Casey, and for every one we catch, there are ten more to take his place. We're fighting a never-ending battle. Booker is always one step ahead of us.

We'll never get him."

"Never say never, Jane." Casey felt Jane's frustration. Sometimes it did feel like a never-ending battle and the stress level was horrendous, but she knew that Jane, like her, could never be happy doing anything else. She glanced at her wristwatch. "Have you eaten?"

"Not yet."

"Come on. I'll buy you lunch. You can tell me all about Stan's near-death experience from his bump on the head," she teased.

"That's the best offer I've gotten all morning," Jane replied, grabbing her jacket.

Chapter Three

"Kami, thanks for letting me stay for a few days." Blaine glanced around the lavishly decorated room. "I do feel out of place in my jeans and T-shirt next to you." She lifted an eyebrow. "You always look like you just stepped off the pages of a fashion magazine." She smiled. "But then again, you've always had class no matter what you were wearing."

"I'm glad you decided to stay. You can stay as long as you'd like. I want you to be comfortable here." She returned Blaine's smile. "And don't sell yourself short, Blaine. You have more class than you give yourself credit for."

Blaine made a face. "I only wish."

"It's true. Would I lie to you? Now stop putting yourself down." She put a finger to her brow. "I've got a great idea. Tomorrow after you get off work let's go shopping for some new clothes for you. I'll take you to a new shop I found last week. You'll love it!"

"It sounds like fun, but you know I don't have your kind of money," she quickly reminded her. "I'm lucky I can make my monthly rent."

Kami shrugged. "Don't worry about it. It'll be my treat."

Blaine pushed a loose strand of hair from her brow. "I can't let you do that."

"You won't accept a gift from your best friend?"

"Kami, you've already done more than enough by letting me stay here."

"I really want to do this for you, Blaine. It'll be fun." Kami drew her mouth up into a pout. "Pretty please?"

Blaine laughed. "Okay," she relented. "But on one condition."

Kami's eyes narrowed. "What's that?"

"That I pay you back. It may take awhile, but I insist."

Kami frowned. "We'll talk about that later." She walked over to Blaine and gave her a hug. "I hope you don't mind, but I've invited a friend over for a drink. I've been wanting you to meet him for quite some time."

Blaine cocked an eye. "Sounds serious. You never mentioned you were seeing anyone."

Kami's eyes shifted. "We're just friends. I've known him for a long time. He's anxious to meet you."

"Are you trying to set me up?" Blaine asked warily.

"No. Nothing like that. I just want you to meet him."

She blew her breath out. "Meeting anyone right now is the last thing I want to do."

"I think it'll do you good. It'll take your mind off what happened. We'll just have one drink. I promise."

She shook her head. "Maybe some other time, Kami. I'm not in the mood tonight. I just want to get a good night's sleep."

"I can't cancel at the last minute," Kami insisted.

"Kami, why didn't you ask me first? Just call him and tell him I'll meet him another night."

"It's too late to cancel. He's probably on his way over. I didn't think you'd mind."

Blaine stared hard at her. "Didn't think I'd mind? I

27

don't want to be set up. If I want a man in my life, then I'll find my own." She looked down at her well-worn jeans. "And I'm obviously not dressed for entertaining," she said with a touch of sarcasm.

"You look fine. It's just casual. He won't care how you're dressed. We'll make it an early night," Kami said. "I promise."

"No. If this is how it's going to be, then I'll just go back to my place. You can entertain him since he's your friend."

"What will I tell him?"

"The truth. I'm not interested."

"How can you say that when you haven't even met Josh?"

"At least I know his name now," Blaine replied flippantly.

"You can't leave. I told Detective Jorgan you'd be staying here for a few days."

"Well, tell her I changed my mind. I can take care of myself. I always have."

"Blaine, you won't even ID the thug who possibly attacked you. You're terrified and you know it. Do you really want to go back to your apartment and spend another sleepless night jumping at every little sound?"

Blaine stared at her. Kami was right, but she was still pissed that Kami hadn't at least run it by her before inviting a guest over. And not just any guest, but a man Kami wanted to set her up with. Blaine hated blind dates and Kami knew it, but most importantly, it was inconsiderate of Kami to do it on Blaine's first night here. "I don't, but I will."

Kami threw her hands up. "Okay, you win. Since you're so good at taking care of yourself, don't call me the next time you're afraid to be alone. I tried to help you, but as usual, you're pushing me away like you do everyone who gets too close."

A pained expression crossed Kami's face. As much

as she wanted to deny the truth Blaine couldn't. Kami was right. Kami had been her confidant and was always there whenever Blaine needed help with her never-ending problems. They'd met in high school. They were complete opposites in personality and lifestyles, but they'd bonded like sisters and their differences complemented each other. Kami had disappeared, without explanation, from her life shortly after their high school graduation. When she returned, she'd resumed her friendship with Blaine as though she'd never been gone. Blaine had never questioned her absence and Kami had offered no explanation. Normally, Blaine would have questioned her, but there was something different about Kami, and Blaine had never been able to quite put her finger on what it was.

Blaine's voice softened. "I'm sorry, Kami. I do appreciate everything you've done for me. I have no right to expect you to put your life on hold every time I have a problem." She cleared her throat. "You have always been there for me. I suppose it wouldn't kill me to do something for you."

"Does that mean you're staying?" Kami asked.

Blaine nodded. "Yes, I'm staying."

"Great!" Kami squeezed Blaine's hand. She jumped when the intercom buzzed. She hurried over to it. "Yes, John."

"Mr. Barnes is on his way up."

"Thank you, John."

Blaine slowly let her breath out. "Look, I'll go to my room, Kami. I don't want to ruin your evening. I can meet him some other time, okay? Besides, I'm tired. Please make my apologies to him."

"No. You have to stay."

Blaine looked at her in surprise. "Why?"

"I want you to meet him right now—tonight, that's

all." She fidgeted with her bracelet. "Just for a few minutes. Please?"

"Okay, but then you're on your own." She walked to a comfortable-looking upholstered antique chair and seated herself.

"He's here," Kami whispered when she heard the familiar knock on the door. She rushed to answer it. Seconds later she led the tall, slim, good-looking man into the living room. Blaine noticed that he was several years older than Kami and her. She definitely wasn't into older men.

"Blaine, I'd like you to meet Josh Barnes," Kami said with a warm smile aimed at Blaine.

Before Blaine could acknowledge him, his eyes locked with hers making her uncomfortable. There was something about his eyes that caused her to instantly distrust him. She definitely wouldn't be going out with him.

"Well, well, she's even better than I imagined, Kami." He smiled, showing off a perfect set of white teeth. "Good work." He moved closer to Blaine. "Stand up," he said softly, extending a hand to help her to her feet.

She cocked a suspicious eye at him. "Why?"

"Because I asked you to," he answered in the same soft voice.

Blaine smirked, shooting a sideways glance at Kami as she noted Josh's expensive suit and the ease with which he wore it. She assumed that his classic movie star looks and obvious wealth made him think he could demand whatever he wanted whenever he wanted it. "Who do you think you are?" Her voice was icy. "No offense, Kami, but I am definitely not impressed. Someone should have taught your friend some proper manners."

Josh kept his eyes on her as his lips turned up into an

amused, but at the same time, eerie smile.

"Just do as he asks," Kami said in a low voice.

Blaine's eyes narrowed. "Why should I?" Her voice dripped with sarcasm. "I don't know who you think you are, but you certainly don't impress me." She folded her arms across her chest.

Josh laughed. "We're going to get to know one another very well before this night is over."

"I don't think so," she replied disgustedly. "Maybe you're used to women throwing themselves at your feet, but I'm not one of them. I am definitely not interested in anything you have to offer."

He inched closer. "I don't give a damn what you are or are not interested in." His eyes traveled over her body. "It's not your brain I'm interested in at this point, but it would serve you well to use it."

His leering eyes sickened her. She couldn't believe he was actually a friend of Kami's. And she definitely couldn't believe that Kami would try to set her up with this obnoxious jerk. She flippantly tossed her head back. "I said I'm not interested." Her voice was as cold as her eyes.

He grabbed her shoulders digging his fingers into her soft flesh. "Listen, baby, I call the shots here. You'd better learn that real fast. Now stand up!" he ordered.

Blaine looked into his steely eyes. "Are you on drugs or something? Get your filthy hands off me!" She slapped at him. "Kami, he needs to go now! If he doesn't then I'm calling the police."

Kami paled. "You can't call the police, Blaine. Just do as he says," she whispered. "Please just do as he says for both our sakes."

"What the hell's going on?" she demanded. "Kami, are

you involved in something illegal with him?"

"Please, Blaine, do what he asks."

"You'd do well to listen to your friend, Blaine. I haven't got all night," Josh spat out bitterly as his fingertips dug deeper into her shoulders. "Now stand up!"

The evil look in his eyes, the same evil look that had been in the eyes of her attacker, sent icy chills through her. She shakily stood, her legs barely supporting her weight as his unsettled eyes bore into every inch of her flesh. She was vulnerable and didn't know what to do. She felt like she'd been stripped naked and forced to stand in front of him while he inspected her. Fear gripped her heart. This couldn't be happening. Not here in Kami's beautiful upscale apartment.

"That's more like it," he said releasing his grip on her. "Nice," he smiled as he walked slowly around her. He slipped an arm around her waist, drawing her close. "Very nice."

His hot, quick breath on her face gagged her. She avoided his eyes as she struggled to free herself from him. "What the hell is this? Get your filthy hands off me!"

"What's the matter, baby?" Josh taunted. "Don't play hard to get with me. I know what you want." His eyes blazed. "You're all the same. You all want the same thing." He sneered. "And I'm the one who'll give it to you. Be good to me and you'll see what I'll do for you."

"I won't be bought!" She placed her hands on his chest and shoved him with all the strength she possessed. "Get away from me! You make me sick to my stomach!" She soon found out that she was no match for his strength.

He grabbed her wrists. "Don't play games with me!"

"Kami, please do something," she screamed. "Don't just stand there, dammit! Call the police now!"

Kami stood silently ignoring her pleas for help.

"Help me, for God's sake!" she pleaded. "What's the matter with you? I'm your friend."

She blinked back tears. "I'm sorry, Blaine." She turned to Josh. "She doesn't know. I didn't tell her," she cried. "Please let her go, Josh. She doesn't *know*."

His nostrils flared angrily and his green eyes flamed. He abruptly released Blaine and walked with long strides to where Kami stood. He grabbed her arms roughly.

"You didn't tell her?" His jaw clenched.

Blaine watched in horror as Josh twisted Kami's arms like she was a rag doll instead of flesh and bones. She was sure he would either break Kami's arms or tear them out of their sockets. "What don't I know, Kami?" she demanded. "Tell me! I deserve to know."

"Josh, let go. You're hurting me!" Kami sobbed. "You're going to break my arms."

"I know," he taunted. "You need to learn your lesson. You were given an order and you've disobeyed." He turned her around until she was facing Blaine. "Now tell her! Tell her how you can afford this expensive lifestyle. Tell her how she might someday have the same if she does as she's told." His eyes darkened. "And tell her the consequences if she refuses."

Blaine looked at Kami. Tears were streaming down her cheeks. Josh still had a tight grip on her arms. The realization of what he meant sank in. "No!" Blaine screamed, running toward the foyer.

Josh threw Kami to the floor, and then lunged for Blaine. "You're not going anywhere," he panted as he yanked her, kicking and screaming back into the living room.

She shrieked as she clawed at his face. "Let me go!"

"I'm so sorry, Blaine," Kami sobbed. "I didn't mean for this to happen." Tears dampened her cheeks. "I had no

33

choice, Blaine. He forced me to do this. Please believe me. I tried to protect you from this."

Blaine stared at her through terror-stricken eyes. "Why?" she asked in a raspy voice. "Why, Kami?"

"Our clients will love you, Blaine," Josh whispered seductively. "But I get the first taste." He smacked his lips together. "And I'm sure it'll be well worth it."

Blaine froze. This time there would be no Good Samaritan passing by to come to her rescue. If Kami refused to help her, then who would? She was trapped. Now she longed to be back in her own apartment. Why had she come here? Kami's apartment was to provide safety, but she'd been lured here under false pretenses and unless she could get out, was about to face unbearable horror at the hands of this monster. "No! You can't make me do this!" She kicked and scratched at him.

"Can't I?" he laughed as he picked her up in his strong arms. "I think you're going to love it, baby."

"Call the police, Kami!" Blaine screamed, trying to free herself. "Please!"

"I'm sorry, Blaine," she cried. "I can't."

"No!" Blaine shrieked.

****

Blaine's bloodcurdling screams echoing down the hallway sickened Kami. With shaky hands, she poured herself a brandy, and then walked over to the sofa. She tried to block out Blaine's muffled cries by turning on the television. She hated herself for betraying Blaine. Blaine trusted her. She didn't deserve this. She'd neither wanted it nor asked for it. She was unaware what awaited her after tonight. She was fragile and Kami doubted Blaine would survive. What was it about Blaine that had caused Josh to throw caution to the wind and take what she hadn't wanted to give? The other girls had all willingly joined his organization. The girls always knew to toe the line where Josh was concerned. Many of his clients were men in high positions and would protect him at any cost so as not to be found out. The girls were well taken care of, came and went freely just as long as Josh was aware of their every movement.

Even though some of them eventually wanted out, that would never happen. There was no way out, so they remained until they were of no further use to him. What had happened to them? She'd assumed they'd moved far away distancing themselves from Josh. Now she wondered. He'd changed. A shiver ran up her spine. Now a woman had no choice but to be forced into the organization. Would Blaine receive the same freedoms Kami did? She doubted it. He'd keep a close eye on her.

If Blaine didn't obey Josh, he would kill them both and he would get away with it. He had no conscience, at least not like normal people did. Someone's suffering and pain didn't affect him in the least. He only cared about his own well-being. He was brutally cold and heartless, and there was no way Kami could protect her friend since she'd never been able to protect herself. She was trapped—they were both trapped—and Josh would never set them free.

****

Casey sat behind the steering wheel, staring out into the darkness. A lone streetlight cast an eerie shadow on the building she was watching. The car was hidden from anyone entering or exiting the building. "Dammit," she complained. "It's starting to rain."

Jane zipped her raincoat. "No surprise. It did call for rain tonight, Casey." She stretched, and then peered out of the window. "We've been here for over an hour. Are you sure Booker's going to show?"

"If he holds true to form, he will. I've followed him here for the past three nights." She lit a cigarette.

Jane grabbed her arm. "I thought you gave those up for good a couple of months ago."

Casey shrugged. "I did, but you know how hard it is. Pressure."

Jane grimaced. "Fine, I'm not going to lecture you anymore," she said distastefully. "Ruin your health, smell up your car, your clothes and hair." She turned her attention back to the window craning her neck as she peered into the misty night. "Don't come crying to me when your lungs give out."

Casey grinned, then blew out a puff of smoke. "I'm sure I won't."

Jane turned slightly and glanced at Casey. "But I will lecture you about something else." She wagged a slender finger in front of Casey's nose.

Casey sighed. "What, mother?"

"You know that you shouldn't have tailed Booker by yourself. If Lt. Richardson finds out he'll have your head." She frowned disapprovingly. "One of these days you're going to get into a real mess and no one will be there to get you out!"

"You were too busy to help. Someone had to do it." She noted Jane's uneasiness. "Let's change the subject," she said lightly. She knew that Jane had her best interests at heart, but sometimes her mothering smothered Casey. When something needed doing, she did it and never worried about the consequences.

"Okay," Jane agreed with a nod, just don't do it again. But if you really have to, get someone from the department to join you." She was quiet for a minute. "You need to start dating seriously again."

Casey looked at her in surprise. "Think of another topic."

"What about Greg?" Jane persisted.

"What about him?" she asked.

"Could he be potential—"

"We're just friends," Casey replied cutting her off. She crushed out her cigarette as her eyes stayed focused on the building.

"Come on. You like him. And I think it goes deeper than friendship. So why not tell him you'd like to take things further?" Jane asked.

"Who said I want to take things further? I—" Casey began, and then abruptly stopped as something caught her attention. A hazy figure approached the building. "Get down, it's Booker," Casey whispered. Two more silhouetted figures quickly joined the first one.

"Are you sure?"

"I'll stake my life on it."

"I'll call for backup," Jane said.

"Not yet," Casey replied. "I'll tell you when."

Casey quietly opened the car door, crouched low, and with her gun poised made her way to the other side of the car.

Jane cautiously raised her head observing Booker's actions. He handed a package to one of the men. She held her breath, waiting until Casey was ready to make her move before exiting the car. One wrong move and it could cost Casey her life and maybe her own as well. She slowly eased herself out of the car, and Casey and she silently crept a safe distance behind the men, the shadows hiding them.

Booker put his hand up to silence the men and tilted

his head, listening. He pulled a gun from his pocket. "You set me up," he snarled.

Jane held her breath. Had Booker heard them? She nudged Casey.

"No, we didn't," one of the men replied. "I swear."

"Throw your guns down," he ordered. "Now!"

The men quickly pulled their guns from their pockets. The shorter man immediately tossed his gun, but the other one slowly lowered his hand and then quickly brought it back up.

Booker fired before the man could take aim. He fell with a thud to the ground. The shorter man ducked, then rolled on the gravel and reached for his gun, which was inches from his fingers. Booker stood over him. He kicked the gun out of the way. "Bad move," he said. He fired catching the man in the side of his head.

"Let's take him," Casey whispered. "He doesn't know there's two of us."

"I'll cover you," Jane said.

Casey quietly made her way until she stood a couple of feet behind Booker. "Drop your weapon, Booker!" Jane ordered.

He turned, startled, but quickly regained his composure. "Looks like we have a standoff," he sneered. He raised his gun and pointed it at her forehead. "Let's see who's the better shot. It sure as hell won't be a cop. Especially one who isn't even smart enough to raise her weapon." He laughed mockingly. "Too bad. Now you don't have a chance."

Casey kept her eyes level with his. "Really, Booker?"

"Really. It's too bad you made a stupid move. Who tipped you off? Those two losers?" he said motioning with his head to the fallen men. He kept his eyes glued to Casey. "It doesn't matter. Any last words?"

Jane fired, catching Booker in the arm. His gun fell to the ground as he clutched his arm. "What the hell?"

"Who's stupid, Booker? Did you really think I'd come alone?"

Jane rushed over to where he stood. "You're under arrest, Booker." She patted him down while reading him his rights. Casey kept her gun trained on him while Jane cuffed him.

"This is police brutality," he said.

Casey nodded toward the dead men on the ground. "And that's murder."

Rain splashed on Booker's head and dripped down his face. "I'm going to bleed to death. Are you going to let me die?"

"I'll call it in," Jane said. She looked at Booker. "The bullet only grazed you. You'll live."

Casey slowly walked around the man. "Was it worth it, Booker?" she asked. "Do you know how many kids you've destroyed? How many families you've torn apart?"

He cocked his head. "Not my problem."

"It is now."

Chapter Four

Kami looked up when Josh walked back into the living room forty-five minutes later. His face was blotched and scratched. Zigzagged lines of dried blood peppered his face.

"Where's Blaine?" she asked in a wobbly voice. If he looked like that, Blaine would be in worse condition. She dreaded his answer.

"Get me something to put on these scratches," he ordered. "That little bitch learned her lesson!"

"Josh, what did you do to her?" She tried to imagine what condition he'd left her in. "Does she need medical help?"

"Do I look stupid?" He scowled at her. "I only gave her what she had coming to her." He eyed Kami suspiciously. "You're not getting soft on me, now are you?"

"I wasn't friends with any of the other girls. Blaine *is* my friend. She didn't want this."

His eyes grew as cold as his voice. "That's what you get for needing friends. Friends only fuck up your life. Now get me something to put on these scratches," he snapped. "My face feels like it's on fire. Now!"

Kami quietly walked into the bathroom and grabbed some antiseptic and cotton balls and set them on the bathroom counter. She caught her reflection in the mirror. She hated herself. Blaine would hate her, too, for what she'd done and she certainly couldn't blame her. Blaine deserved a full explanation. She wouldn't understand, but Kami would do her best to let her know that dragging her into this mess was not her intention and something she'd tried to avoid doing. She should have refused and taken the consequences. Or maybe she should have told someone. But the cops wouldn't understand either. How could they when she'd had every opportunity to escape and go for help, but didn't. She'd chosen to stay. Even though everyone would assume it was out of greed for her life of luxury, they would never understand that she only stayed out of fear. She'd never be free of Josh. She took a ragged breath as she splashed cold water on her face.

****

Later after Kami had attended to Josh's injuries and he'd left, she tiptoed to the bedroom and quietly stepped inside. "He's gone," she said in a barely audible voice. She cringed when she saw Blaine's swollen eyes and mouth. She reached out a hand, as the words she longed to say stayed clogged in her throat. What could she say? No words could ease the pain and humiliation of what Blaine had just endured.

Blaine sat on the edge of the bed. "Stay away from me," she choked, shrugging off Kami's hand. "I thought we were friends — almost like sisters." Her eyes glistened with tears. "I can't believe you set me up like this, Kami. What did I ever do to you to deserve this? I trusted you. You were my best friend." Her voice cracked before breaking. "You knew this was going to happen. That's why you invited me to stay. It had nothing to do with you caring about my safety. I'm getting out of here."

"You can't go, Blaine," she murmured. "I'm so sorry. You have to stay. This is your home now."

41

"I don't know what you're talking about. I'm going back to my apartment."

"That's a bad idea," Kami replied.

"No. It's the only choice I have." She swallowed hard. "I can't believe you did this to me. How could you? I never want to see you again, Kami. The quicker I get away from you, the better off I'll be." She winced. "I'll never understand how you can even be friends with someone who abused me almost in front of you. What's wrong with you, Kami?" she shrieked. "How could you let him do this to me and do nothing to help me? Tell me! Why?"

"Josh Barnes isn't my friend, Blaine." She ran her hand through her tangled hair. "It's complicated." She sighed tiredly. "I'll try to explain it to you, but I don't think you'll understand just what he's capable of."

Blaine grabbed a tissue from the box on the bedside table and dabbed at her mouth "What's complicated about it, Kami? You invited him here tonight to rape me. That's sick! How much did he pay you to lure me here?"

Kami cringed. She was hurt by Blaine's accusations, but knew that she couldn't blame her for anything she said or did from this moment on. She'd been brutally violated in the worst possible way.

"How much?" Blaine persisted.

Kami's eyes brimmed with tears. "Don't be ridiculous." She tensed. "Listen to me, please. I don't know how to explain this to you, but I'll try."

"Nothing you say can undo what's been done."

"Josh owns you now, Blaine. You're his girl—his exclusive property—until he decides if and when to share you," she cried. "Don't you see? I had no choice and I never wanted you to become involved in this. But once Josh Barnes sets his mind on something, there's no stopping him."

"What are you talking about, Kami? Nobody owns me." Her eyes narrowed as she looked into Kami's haunted eyes. "What's really going on?"

Tears rolled down Kami's face. "How did you possibly think that I could afford all of this?" she asked, throwing her arms up. "Are you that naive? A private secretary doesn't make enough to afford this kind of luxury or to live in an apartment in this neighborhood. Josh owns this building and everyone in it." She took a deep breath. "I sell my body for money. You deserve to know the truth. Surely you must have wondered about all the nights I told you I was busy and especially the obvious fact that I never had a steady man in my life. I couldn't."

Blaine stared in disbelief. "I don't want to hear any more," she moaned, placing her hands over her ears. "Get away from me! You make me sick."

Kami grabbed her hands and held them tightly. "You have to listen to me!" she pleaded. "I belong to Josh and so do the other girls and there is nothing we can do about it! Don't you think we've tried? If there was a way to get out, I would have done it a long time ago."

"What does any of this have to do with me? He raped me, Kami, and I'll be damned if he's going to get away with it! I've been violated enough and I'm taking charge of my life starting now! I'm having charges filed against him."

Kami bit her bottom lip. "Josh wanted some new blood in the organization to keep his clients satisfied. He was afraid if they became bored they'd go elsewhere. He knew we were friends so I was instructed — no, *forced* — to lure you into it, but I couldn't," she stammered, ashamed with her deceit. "I kept putting him off until I couldn't any longer."

"Kami, you deliberately set me up. And that's the only reason you wanted me to stay here. Admit it."

"No, Blaine." She shook her head. "I care too much about you. You've been through so many horrible things in your life. I tried to explain that to Josh, but he refused to listen."

Blaine stood, glared at Kami, and took a few steps toward the door. She turned and looked over her shoulder at Kami. "You knew what he was doing to me and you didn't try to stop him." Her chin quivered. "How could you just sit in the living room and do nothing? I'm calling the police!"

"No." She rushed over to Blaine. "I told you...you can't."

She pushed Kami out of the way. "I can and I will."

Kami grabbed her arm. "Don't! He'll kill us both if you do." She drew a shaky breath. "You know what he's capable of." She peered into Blaine's eyes.

Blaine studied her. "You're serious, aren't you?"

She slowly nodded. "Deadly serious. What he did to you is mild compared to the evil he's capable of."

Blaine shivered involuntarily. "Kami, there has to be a way out. He can't get away with this."

She looked desperately at Blaine. "There's no way out. If there was, I would have gotten out a long time ago. Do you think I want to live like this for the rest of my life? I can't date, have anyone over, or do any of the normal things everyone takes for granted. This is like a prison."

Blaine blinked hard. "He has no right—"

"That's just it. He lives by his own rules." She swallowed the lump in her throat. "I'm sorry, Blaine, for what I've allowed to happen to you. You of all people never deserved this."

"I don't think I'll ever be able to forgive you, Kami, but

right now we've got to figure this mess out. I still think there has to be a way. Who the hell does Josh Barnes think he is?"

"God," Kami whispered. "He thinks he's God."

Blaine shuddered.

"Let me help you clean yourself up. You must be in so much pain." She winced at Blaine's bruised face.

She numbly nodded. "I don't know which is worse—the physical or emotional pain."

****

Lt. Richardson smiled widely. "I want to congratulate you two on your fine work tonight." He peered at Casey. "There is one little thing, though, Jorgan."

"Yes, Lt. Richardson?" Casey smiled smugly as she leaned back in her chair.

"Don't you ever tail a suspect again without backup," he warned, pointing a finger under her nose. "You could have gotten yourself killed."

"I had a hunch where he might be. I wanted to check it out. I would never confront any potential suspect without backup," she explained. "I knew Jane would be with me when everything came down."

"Don't do it again. Next time you run it by me first."

"Yes, sir. It won't happen again," she promised with a mischievous glint in her eye.

He eyed her sharply. "See that it doesn't. I'm the one who has to answer for my detectives' actions." He turned to leave, then stopped and looked at them with another broad smile. "Just the same, nice work, detectives."

Casey kept her gaze focused on him as he slowly made his way back to his office. He was a lonely man and his detectives were the only family he had. He'd sacrificed a twenty-year marriage for the job. She'd gotten to know Mrs. Richardson fairly well through the years and what eventually became apparent to her obviously didn't to Lt. Richardson. The stress proved too much, and in the end she'd grown too lonely to live with a man who was constantly on call, and when he was home, too tired to pay her much notice. Casey knew that he loved his wife deeply and probably always would. She had watched in pained silence as the shock of his divorce left him bewildered and more intent to bury himself in his work.

She understood only too well the terrible loneliness of suddenly being single again. What had kept her preoccupied through her long and endless nights, though, was the knowledge that somewhere out there she had a younger sister. She'd spent several years and a small fortune tracking down leads that in the end only left her feeling more despondent with each dead end. Until one day a lead gave her a last name. A couple named Kirsten had adopted Blaine, but they were both deceased. She'd contacted everyone she could find with the surname Kirsten, but reached a dead end there, too. None of them were related to Blaine's family. It was as though Blaine had vanished off the face of the earth. Casey realized that there was a possibility that Blaine wasn't even alive, but she refused to accept it. Death records had turned up nothing, which gave her renewed hope. She'd never give up her quest, knowing deep within her heart that her sister was out there somewhere and she'd find her. Now that she had, her dreams of a happy reunion were dashed. She had to keep that news from Blaine…at least for now.

When Casey saw Blaine for the first time, there was no doubt in her mind that she'd finally found her long lost sister. She was a younger version of their mother. Blaine had shown no recognition of her, but then she'd been too young to remember Casey or their parents. She'd grown up with a family. Casey was surprised, though, seeing Blaine's shabby apartment and dire living conditions. Obviously, something had gone wrong in her life. Casey had hoped Blaine's life would have been the stuff fairy-tales were made of. Now, knowing Blaine had been viciously attacked left a bitter taste in Casey's mouth. It was almost more than she could bear, but she had to keep her emotions under control.

Jane's eyes narrowed. "Something wrong?" she asked. "You look deep in thought."

Casey looked up. "No, I'm just a little tired. I need to finish up some paperwork before calling it a night."

"I'll help," Jane offered. "It'll go quicker."

"No, I can do it. Go home and surprise Stan."

"I don't mind," Jane protested. "And Stan won't either."

"No, really. I can do it. Go home, put on some sexy lingerie, and shock Stan."

Jane laughed. "He'd probably have a coronary. But it would be nice to get out of here at a decent hour for a change."

"Have fun because tomorrow will be busy."

Jane lifted an eyebrow. "Isn't every day?"

"Unfortunately. Crime never stops."

Casey's cell phone buzzed and she held up a finger. "Hold that thought." She took the call. "Hi, Matt. Did you find anything?" she asked. "Yes! Thank you." She ended the call and grinning turned her attention back to Jane.

"Are you going to tell me what's suddenly got you so excited?"

"We need to pay a visit to Blaine Kirsten tomorrow morning. She's got to come down here and make a positive ID. This news should make her happy — I'm positive now that the two attacks are related after all."

"What happened?"

"The perp we're holding for the attack on that teenager had some of Blaine's personal effects on him."

"Why are we just finding out about this now?"

"Matt said it was an oversight when he was being processed. He's been questioned about how he happened to have some of Blaine Kirsten's possessions, and the idiot claims he doesn't know how he got them."

"Maybe he found them or someone gave them to him?"

Casey screwed up her face. "Now what do you think?"

"You're right. But we need to emphasize to Blaine that he'll walk on her attack without being identified by her."

"I think that will be enough to convince her and close the file on this one."

"Perfect way to end my shift," Jane replied with a smile as she grabbed her purse and jacket.

****

Kami nervously sipped a second cup of coffee. A loud knock at the door startled her. She set her cup down, slowly stood, and moved to the door. She wondered why John had let someone up unannounced. She'd make sure he heard about it. Even when Josh was visiting, John always notified her. "Who's there?" she asked apprehensively.

"Detectives Jorgan and Adams. We need to speak to Blaine."

Kami recognized the voice as Detective Jorgan's. She wrapped her pale blue robe tighter around herself. "She can't talk to you right now," she called through the door.

"Miss Matthews, we have a photo we would like her to look at," Casey persisted. "Is she here?"

"What's going on, Kami?" Blaine asked, walking into the entrance hall. "Who's here?" she asked worriedly.

"Nothing's wrong. Go back to bed or get some coffee," she whispered. "I'll handle this."

"Miss Matthews," Casey persisted. "This is important."

Blaine shot Kami a hard look as her eyebrows slightly raised. "Let her in," she demanded.

"Blaine, look at yourself. What will we say happened?" Kami asked nervously.

She shrugged her shoulders. "I should just tell them the truth about your *friend*," she said sarcastically. "I've had all night to think about it."

Kami chewed her bottom lip. "I told you, you can't," she hissed. Blaine's fresh bruises would need an explanation.

"Miss Matthews, is everything all right?" Casey called.

"Give me a minute." She turned to Blaine. She had to convince her to act as normally as possible. "Look, if you tell them, what makes you think they'll believe you? Doesn't it seem odd that you would be attacked twice in the same week? The cops will think you're lying about both attacks. Especially since you refused to help your own case in the first attack. Besides, it'll be your word against his, and I can't risk siding with you so please don't ask me to." She saw Blaine's jaw twitch. "And then what do you think he'll do to you for talking about him to the police?"

"What about my bruises?" Blaine asked dejectedly. "How do we explain them?"

"I don't know. Say you fell or something. Okay?"

"I don't have a choice."

"You really don't." Kami opened the door. "I'm sorry for the delay," she said pasting a brief smile on her lips.

Casey nodded as she observed Blaine who stood next to Kami. "What happened to you?" Her eyes narrowed.

"I was in an accident," Blaine answered.

"When?" Casey asked with a sideways glance at Jane.

"Look, Detective, you said you have a photo to show her," Kami interrupted.

"Yes, we do. May we come in?" Jane's voice was quiet. She shot a warning look at Casey.

"Be my guest." Kami flung the door wide open.

"I'm Detective Jane Adams," Jane said following Casey into the foyer.

Blaine and Kami nodded, but kept silent.

Casey pulled a photograph from her pocket and thrust it at Blaine. "Look at this guy. Is he the one who attacked you?"

Blaine took the picture and carefully studied it. Casey saw the fear come into her eyes at the sight of her attacker. "Yes, that's him," she replied weakly. She returned the picture to Casey. "What happens now?" Her lips were drawn tight.

"He had some of your possessions on him. We need you to come down to the station," Jane said.

"What for? This is the bastard who attacked me. And if he had my stuff, that should be proof enough. I've done my part, now it's up to you to make sure he stays locked up."

"It's not. And even if it was, you still need to make a positive identification and sign a statement," Jane replied calmly.

"But it proves he attacked me since he had my stuff."

"He denying it…says he found it."

"He's a liar." Blaine frowned. "When would I have to come down?"

"Now would be good. The sooner you do it, the quicker we can put him away."

"Now?" She inhaled sharply.

"It's as good a time as any," Jane said, and then added, "We can wait until you dress and then drive you down to the precinct. We'll bring you back when you're finished."

She put a hand to her face. "I'm sure you two can see that I'm in no condition to go anywhere at the moment. Maybe in a day or two when my bruises fade some."

"It'll only take a few minutes," Casey said.

"You heard Blaine. She's been through enough lately. She'll come down to the station in a few days," Kami stated as she kept her eyes closely riveted on Blaine. "I'll drive her."

Casey observed the look that passed between Blaine and Kami. They were hiding something. But what? She was certain of one thing as she studied Blaine. She hadn't been in any accident. Kami Matthews knew what had happened to her and was the key. The woman was too quick to jump in with the answers before Blaine had a chance to even open her mouth. Matthews was afraid to let Blaine speak for herself, and Casey was determined to find out why. She needed to get Blaine alone. She'd try to gain her trust and then convince her to talk. That was the only hope she had to learn the truth about her supposed accident. She couldn't bear seeing her sister's beautiful face bruised and swollen. She swallowed hard trying to keep her anger under control.

"A few days may be too late. We can only hold him for so long, then he's back on the streets," Casey warned. "His next victim might not be so lucky, Blaine."

"Why don't you get that teenager to sign a statement?" Blaine asked. "At least you can hold him for her rape. Why me?"

"She's frightened. What happened to her could have happened to you, Blaine."

"And I'm not?" she countered.

Casey quickly lost control over her emotions. "Oh, you're frightened all right, but of something else." She stared evenly at her. "What's going on?"

Blaine laughed sarcastically. "What else could I possibly be afraid of? Isn't being mugged and roughed up enough?"

"You tell us. You were beaten again, Blaine," Casey stated. "Those bruises were not the result of an accident."

"So you're a doctor, too, Detective?" Blaine's eyes darkened.

"I think you'd better leave," Kami said. "I'll bring her down to the police department in a few days."

Casey ignored her comment and caught Jane's eye.

"How can you afford this apartment, Miss Matthews?" Jane asked.

"I'm a private secretary," Kami calmly answered. "Not that it's any of your business."

Jane lifted an eyebrow. "I didn't know secretaries made that much money these days. Especially to be able to afford to live in this neighborhood."

"A good one does," she snapped. "Besides, it's really none of your business where I get my money," she said coldly as she held the door wide. "I have nothing further to say to you."

Jane shook her head as she turned toward Blaine. "It's Blaine we came to speak to."

Casey gently laid a hand on Blaine's shoulder. "You don't deserve whatever's going on in your life right now, Blaine. You owe it to yourself to at least put this animal away," she said softly. "It'll just take a few minutes of your time. No one deserves what happened to you."

Blaine was silent. Her lip trembled slightly. She opened her mouth to speak, but then quickly closed it.

Casey sensed Blaine's resolve was breaking. She needed to talk to her alone without Kami's interference.

Blaine's eyes nervously shifted.

"Leave her alone!" Kami demanded aiming a dirty look at Casey. "Get out of my apartment this minute or I'll have both your badges."

"This concerns Blaine. Stay out of it," Jane ordered, turning to Kami.

"This happens to be my apartment," Kami shot back. "You have no right to speak to me this way in my own home."

"You're a smart woman, Blaine," Casey continued. "We're on your side. Whatever's going on right now, we can help."

Blaine looked at the three women surrounding her, her gaze finally resting on Casey. "Leave me alone, please," she said in a low voice.

Casey's jaw briefly tightened, then relaxed. "Okay, fine. I hope you know what you're doing." She turned to leave, then looking once more at Blaine, said, "You know where to reach us."

Blaine choked back tears. "I'm sorry."

Casey pulled a card and a pen from her pocket. She scribbled something on it, and then thrust it into Blaine's trembling hand. "Here's my private cell phone number. Call me day or night. You probably don't believe this, but I care." She glanced at Jane. "We both care."

****

"What do you think?" Jane asked as they drove toward the station.

Casey gripped the steering wheel. "I don't know." She took a hand from the steering wheel and rubbed her eyes. "She's covering something up. But what and why?" She sighed. "Who is she protecting? Someone beat the shit out of her. I wonder if it's connected with the scumbag we're holding — maybe a warning to her."

Jane frowned. "No, I don't think so."

"Why?"

"It's too obvious, Casey." Jane ran her hand through her short black hair. "Kami Matthews is running scared and Blaine is covering for *her*."

Casey frowned. "You think Kami beat her up? Come on, get serious," she chuckled. "I don't think so."

She shook her head. "No, don't be ridiculous. Not Kami. Just think for a minute. Kami is on the defense. She knows who did this to Blaine and my gut instinct tells me that she's involved…I feel it. Let's run a check on her. See if she has any dark secrets in her past."

"Why doesn't Blaine tell us what really happened then? She had the opportunity to spill her guts and get the hell out of there."

"Think about it, Casey. Put yourself in Blaine's shoes. She's scared…too scared to risk talking to us. Who knows what kind of threats Kami Matthews has made or been forced to make to Blaine."

Casey thought about it for a minute. "Makes sense." She pulled into a parking space. "Let's see if anything comes up on Kami Matthews."

****

"They don't believe us, Kami." Blaine paced back and forth across the living room carpet.

"Sure they do," Kami answered confidently. "They were trying to trick you into talking."

"They're detectives, remember. They'll be back." She thought she'd seen genuine concern in Detectives Adams' and Jorgan's eyes. She was certain that she hadn't imagined it. Her common sense told her that they were two cops just doing their job and didn't care about her as a person. She was just a case to be solved and that was all. After all, what did they really know or care about her life and the hell she'd been living all these years? Their only concern was with making their collar. She stopped pacing and looked at Kami. She could never forgive her for subjecting her to Josh Barnes. Their friendship was over and she felt only contempt for her now. It crushed her. Their renewed friendship had only been a ruse, and Blaine couldn't believe what a fool she'd been to allow herself to be taken in. She was just a new recruit for Josh Barnes and in the end, she had meant nothing to Kami. She would get out of this mess — she'd find a way. She looked at the card Detective Jorgan had given her.

"Give me that, Blaine."

"Why should I?" Her eyes were icy.

Kami licked her lips. "Look, I know I dragged you into this. I'm sorry, but what else could I do?" She twisted a strand of long blonde hair around her finger. "All I can say is that I'm sorry." Her lips drew up into a pout. "Hate me all you want, but I'm trying to save your life. Someday maybe you'll realize that."

Blaine looked at her former friend's beautiful face refusing to see the pain in her eyes. "I'll bet you are. How much do you get for bringing in new girls? What's your cut? You and Josh Barnes have quite an operation going, don't you?" She glared at her. "You two deserve what you get. I hope you both burn in hell." Her voice was cold. "He will be stopped one way or the other. This is my chance and I'm going to take it. I may never get another opportunity. I should have told the detectives the truth when they were here."

"I'm warning you, Blaine, forget about turning Josh in. If you do, you'll end up dead." She snatched the card from

Blaine's hand. "You can count on it."

"Give it back!" Her eyes flashed.

"It's for your own good," Kami replied as she ripped the card into tiny pieces.

Blaine's eyes filled with tears. "I can't believe you did that. I can't talk to you anymore. I need to be alone."

Kami placed her hands on her hips. "I have a few errands to run. I'll be gone for a few hours." She searched Blaine's eyes. "I know you won't do anything stupid," she said matter-of-factly. "Your life depends on it." She slipped her jacket on. "You can start dinner if I'm not back by five. Josh is bringing a couple of clients over later, so we'll be eating early."

"Kami." Blaine's eyes grew wide. "That bastard raped and beat me last night and now he expects me to be a prostitute for him?" She stared in disbelief at Kami's expressionless face.

"You'll get used to it in time. We all do. Besides, you needn't worry. These guys aren't your average men. These are some very influential men…even politicians." She looked evenly at Blaine. "You won't catch any diseases if that's what you're worried about."

Blaine was stunned. "I can't believe I've known you all this time and never really knew you at all. How could I have been so blind? When you said you had to frequently work nights, I never imagined what kind of work you were doing," she said disgustedly. "Maybe being a prostitute makes you feel good about yourself, but I can't and won't do it!"

"Think what you want to about me, Blaine." She lowered her eyes. "I have to run. See you later."

Blaine waited until she was certain that Kami had gone, and then picked up the phone. Her hand shook so badly she almost dropped it. After she got the Philadelphia

Police Department number from information, she quickly punched in the numbers and punched in some more for the detective's precinct. "I've got to speak to Detective Jorgan. It's an emergency," she said when her call was received. She waited while her call was put through.

"I'm sorry, she's out. Can someone else help you?"

"No...please," Blaine pleaded. "I don't have much time. I need to talk to her."

"Let me get someone else to help you."

"No. Please just tell Detective Jorgan that Blaine Kirsten called." After she hung up, she walked over to an easy chair and sat down, drawing her legs to her chin. She wrapped her arms tightly around her knees and held on as though she were hanging on for her life. "Please call," she whispered as tears poured down her cheeks. She didn't know which was worse, her physical pain or her mental anguish. "How will I ever get out of this mess?" she moaned.

****

Casey threw a couple of files on her desk then sorted through her messages. "Shit!"

"What?" Jane asked watching the color drain from her partner's face.

She handed the message to Jane. "A message to call Blaine Kirsten. That's all it says." She picked up the phone, and after locating Kami's number, quickly dialed. "Come on, answer!" She tapped her pencil against the phone as it continued to ring. "Come on!"

****

Blaine slowly opened her eyes. She hadn't realized she'd fallen asleep. The phone was ringing. She grabbed it on the forth ring right before the answering machine kicked in. "Hello?" she groggily answered.

"It's Detective Jorgan, Blaine. Are you all right?"

"Yes…I think so." She stretched her cramped limbs.

"I'll be right over."

"No, please don't come here."

"Are you in some kind of trouble?"

She hesitated. "Yes…I don't know. Help me, please. I don't know what to do."

"I'm coming over," Casey said with a note of finality in her voice.

"No, please don't do that, Detective Jorgan." Blaine froze as the phone was abruptly ripped from her hand. She hadn't heard the key in the lock or the apartment door opening.

"Blaine is just fine, Detective Jorgan. Now please leave us alone!" Kami set the phone down and then whirled with glaring eyes to face Blaine. "You don't obey too well, do you, Blaine? You're a fool! That detective will get you killed!" She stalked off to the kitchen.

Chapter Five

"What's the matter, Casey?" Jane asked. "Are we going over there or not?" She stood by the side of her desk.

"No…I don't know, Jane." She rested her chin in her hands. "She's in big trouble and there's nothing I can do about it. She called me and asked me to help her, then I'm told to back off!" She slammed her fist on her desk.

"Don't get so emotionally involved, Casey."

"Jane, she's just a kid! I've got to help her. If I don't, I'll never be able to live with myself."

Jane was quiet for a minute. "Why doesn't she want us to come over? What did she say?"

"She asked me to help her and then Matthews grabbed the phone. Matthews is definitely hiding something that she's afraid Blaine will tell us."

"Do you want to go over there to check things out… make sure Blaine's okay?"

Casey rubbed her temples. "You know what will happen. She won't tell us anything as long as Kami Matthews is around." She exhaled loudly. "Did the report on Matthews come back yet?"

"Let me see." Jane shuffled through some papers on her desk. "Here it is…looks clean…works as a secretary for

Pendington Chemical."

"Where do we go from here?" Casey frowned.

Jane was thoughtful for a moment. "We could stake her out."

Casey lifted an eyebrow. "For what purpose? Being a first-class bitch? I don't think there's a law against that."

Jane's eyes narrowed. "Well, we know she's hiding something. Let's do it on our own time—strictly private."

"Wow! I don't believe what I'm hearing! This coming from the woman who gave me hell when I staked out Booker without going through the proper channels."

"This is different. Matthews isn't a suspect in any case we're working on…Booker was an active case."

"I don't know. Lt. Richardson would have our asses if he found out what we were doing whether on our own time or not."

Jane rolled her eyes. "Come on, since when have you followed orders to the letter? Besides, the lieutenant will never know. I'll call Stan and tell him to fix his own dinner." Her eyes twinkled. "Come on, let's do it. What do you say?"

"The last time you told Stan he'd be fixing his own dinner he didn't talk to you for a week and me for an entire month." She smiled. "Remember?"

She laughed. "Don't worry about Stan. He'll survive. A little takeout every now and then never hurt anyone."

Casey eyed her suspiciously. "You never get this passionate about a case. Do you know something I don't?"

Jane impatiently shifted her weight from one foot to the other. "I'm going purely on gut instinct."

Casey jumped to her feet. "That's good enough for me. What are we waiting for? Let's go for it."

****

Josh smiled smugly at Blaine. "Here's our new girl, Mr. James." He affectionately stroked Blaine's arm. "I think you'll find her even better than you imagine."

Arnold James smiled at Blaine. She wanted to vomit as she looked at the bald, fat man. She estimated him to be in his mid-fifties. His friend, Bernard Miller, didn't appear to be in any better physical condition, although he was at least ten years younger.

She was uncomfortable beneath all the makeup Kami had put on her to mask her bruises. Josh had instructed Kami to do whatever it took to camouflage the ugly red welts. She wondered what these men would think of Josh if they knew how they were threatened into submission to perform for them. Would that mean anything to them?

"I'm sticking with my Kami," Bernard said with a broad grin. "You can never go wrong with a sure thing." He winked at Josh.

Kami looked seductively at him as she playfully put her hand on his knee rubbing the bulging flesh. "Shall we have a private party?" she giggled, grabbing his hand.

"You don't have to ask me twice," he replied enthusiastically as he pulled himself to his feet.

Blaine sat stiffly on the sofa looking down at her hands, which were gripped tightly together. She'd never in a million years be able to act so nonchalantly as Kami did. Nor would she want to. These men were no better than Josh. They only had one thing on their minds and it filled her with a boiling rage. They were sick, pathetic men. If the opportunity arose, Blaine intended to turn Josh in no matter what Kami said. Damn the consequences. Death would be better than what she'd been forced into.

"Blaine, Mr. James is one of our most valued clients.

Be nice to him. I promised him that he could be the first with you." He turned to the man. "She'll be okay. I promise. The first time my girls go pro they tend to be a bit nervous." He winked at the man.

"No. I don't want any part of this! I'm not one of your girls. You're forcing me to do this!" Blaine cried. "I'm not some possession you can sell to the highest bidder. I'm a human being for God's sake!"

Arnold James looked uncomfortable. "If there's a problem, then maybe we'd better forget about tonight." His forehead furrowed. "I don't want any trouble." He frowned. "It doesn't look like she's ready, Barnes. The other girls were always willing and eager. You sure she's legit?"

"Everything is legit. My girls wouldn't be here otherwise. Let me talk to her for a moment," he said, grabbing Blaine's hand and pulling her to the hallway.

"I'm not doing it," Blaine said through gritted teeth. "You can't force me to."

Josh's eyes flashed angrily. "You'll do as I say if you know what's good for you," he said through gritted teeth. "The next time you won't live to tell about it!"

Blaine looked into his wild eyes. "You can't force me into prostitution! I'd rather be dead."

"That can be arranged," he snarled. "You'll do as I say. Do you think anyone in the city will even bat an eye if you turn up missing? Girls like you are a dime a dozen. You have no family, Blaine, and it appears you have no friends outside of Kami. Whatever's left of your body after I get done with you will be tossed into a pauper's grave. Do you think the police are going to waste their time with an investigation? Especially without family members putting the heat on?"

The look in his demented eyes told her that he wasn't

joking. He couldn't care less if she lived or died. All he cared about was money. If he killed her, he'd soon find a replacement. Another girl would be forced into this. The only way she could help potential victims was to somehow find a way to put him away for good. She had to stay alive.

"Do I make myself clear?" He grabbed her shoulders and shook her. When she didn't respond, he repeated himself. "I said, do I make myself clear?"

She numbly nodded.

"Good. If you play your cards right, a year from now you can be living in style like your friend Kami. But you have to earn my trust first." He smoothed his tan sport coat. "Let's move it! Mr. James doesn't have all night." He led her back into the living room. "Everything's fine now," he said to the older man. "She's willing to please you no matter what you request."

Blaine stood in silence as Mr. James walked over to her and slipped an arm around her slim waist.

****

"Well, what do you think?" Jane asked.

"I don't know. Just because two men entered the building doesn't mean they were there to see Kami."

"No, it doesn't." Jane drummed her fingertips on the steering wheel. "But I think we need to check on Blaine."

"Let's do it."

The two women got out of the car, walked into the lobby, then hurried over to the elevator and pushed the button for Kami's floor.

"Excuse me, ladies. Whom do you wish to see?"

"Kami Matthews," Casey nonchalantly answered.

"I'm sorry, ladies, but you can't go up to Miss Matthews' apartment without being announced," John brusquely said.

"Is she expecting you?"

Casey looked down at the beige plush carpeting, then back at the man. "Since when do we need to be announced?" she asked. "You weren't around to announce us the other day," she said impatiently.

"That was strictly an oversight on my part, I'm afraid." He flicked a speck of lint from his jacket. "I have my orders from Miss Matthews. She didn't notify me that she was expecting anyone."

"Who are those men who entered the building earlier? What apartment did they go to?"

He raised his eyebrows. "That's none of your business."

"Are you required to announce everyone?" Jane asked.

"That's correct."

"Does Miss Matthews entertain frequently?"

"If she does, I wouldn't know. That's certainly none of my concern. Now shall I announce you or not?"

"Please do." Casey matched his haughtiness. "Tell her Detectives Jorgan and Adams are here to see her."

"Just one moment, please," John said.

Casey watched him as he picked up a handset and pushed a button. After a few seconds, he disconnected the call.

"Miss Matthews does not wish to see you. She requests that you leave Miss Kirsten and her alone," John said as he motioned with a hand toward the exit.

Casey slowly walked over to the man, studying his articulate dress and manners. "It must cost a bundle to live here," she stated.

"It is quite expensive," he admitted. "But then again, you get what you pay for."

Casey tilted her head. "Doesn't it seem odd to you that

a young woman employed as a secretary can afford to live here?"

"I don't question the inhabitants' sources of income. It's none of my business," he retorted.

Casey smiled. "Strictly upper-class." She admired the furnishings in the lobby. "How much do you make a week?"

"I beg your pardon!" He sniffed indignantly. "That is also none of your business!"

She turned to Jane. "Let's go." They walked toward the exit, and then Casey stopped, turned, and looked again at the man. "We'll be back."

****

Josh Barnes closed the door behind the two men, and then turned to Kami. "What do those detectives want?" he snarled.

"They want Blaine to identify the guy who attacked her the other night," Kami answered.

"Well, get rid of them. We don't need them hanging around here!" He carefully studied her. "You're not trying to double cross me, are you?"

"Of course not. You know me better than that, Josh."

"You'd better be telling me the truth," he warned. "Because if I find out you're doing anything behind my back you'll be sorry you were ever born." He counted out some bills and handed them to her. He looked at Blaine. He handed her half the amount he'd given to Kami.

"I don't want that filthy money!" Blaine shouted throwing it back at him. "At least I'll know that I didn't sell my body for sex." She shot a dirty look at Kami.

He laughed. "Take it, baby. You earned it. Mr. Miller tells me you were really something. He wants to make you his number one girl and he's not usually a man who is so easily pleased." He placed his large hands on her shoulders. "After the taste I got, I knew you were perfect for him."

"Fuck you and fuck him! I'm going to the police!" she announced without batting an eye. "You can't force me to do these sick sex acts with your perverted friends! I would rather be dead than to have to live like this for the rest of my life!"

Kami's eyes grew wide with fear. "You don't mean that, Blaine."

"Yes, I do!"

"You may get your wish." He grabbed Blaine's arm, digging his fingers into her tender flesh. "I hope you're kidding because if you're not, that pretty face of yours is going to be permanently disfigured!"

"You'll never own me!" she screamed pulling her arm from his grip.

"Would you like a repeat performance of last night? It can be arranged," he cautioned.

Blaine remained silent.

"I thought so." He turned his attention to Kami. "I've got some business to attend to. Talk some sense into her if you value her life!" He pushed Blaine to the floor. "And your own!"

****

"Turn the heat up, Casey. I'm freezing," Jane said pulling her thin jacket tighter around herself. "I thought it was supposed to be warmer tonight."

Casey threw a sweater at her. "Here, put this on," she said and laughed. "I've never known anyone who complains as much as you do about the weather."

Jane's teeth chattered as she peered through the window. "I think I see him," she whispered excitedly.

Casey looked to where Jane was anxiously pointing a

66

finger. "Let's go!"

****

Kami swallowed hard. "Blaine, please cooperate. You might as well get used to it because it's not going to change. Try to learn to make the best of it. Someday you'll even make as much money as I do and you'll be able to write your own ticket."

"I told him and I'll repeat it for you since you keep blocking it out. Josh Barnes does not own me." Blaine slowly shook her head back and forth. "Kami, can't you understand that if I have to sell my body to get all the material things that you have, then it's worthless to me?" She looked closely at her. "I can't believe you can do this night after night and not feel sick to your stomach." She massaged her throbbing temples. "I just want to forget this horrible nightmare and try to pick up the pieces of my life. I'm going back to my own place. It might not be much, but at least it's mine. Do what you want to with your life, but I hope that someday you'll come to your senses and see what you've lost—your pride and self-esteem."

"Why can't you get it through your thick skull that he *does* own you? You can't go home." Her voice had an air of finality to it. "This is your home now. Josh is having your things brought over tomorrow." She placed her hands on her hips waiting for Blaine's reaction.

Blaine snorted. "He can't do that! Who the hell does he think he is?"

Kami walked slowly over to the sofa and wearily sank into it. She absentmindedly tapped her fingers on the marble-topped coffee table. "I told you before that Josh Barnes thinks he is God and he has the money, power, and connections to do whatever he wants to do. You'll find that out, Blaine, and

67

I hope you don't find it out the hard way. You can't stop him. Don't you think others have tried?" Her voice was low. "You can have all the things you never had as a kid. I won't lie to you, Blaine. Your life will be better if you just go along with him. I'm warning you not to cross him. He's a very dangerous man and just for spite he probably wouldn't have you killed, but disfigured for life in some way." She swallowed the lump in her throat. "I've seen firsthand what he's capable of doing. The beating he gave you is mild compared to what he's done to some of the girls who've betrayed him." Tears filled her eyes as she pleaded with Blaine. "Just listen to me for both our sakes."

"There are laws against what he does," Blaine reasoned. "I don't even know what label to give it. I would say human trafficking, in my case, but he lets you freely come and go. You could have gotten out and saved others from him. You're as bad as he is because you did nothing. He can't get away with this. He's only trying to scare us into going along with him."

"Think what you want. But I don't have as much freedom as you think." She looked into Blaine's eyes. "Some of the same men who make the laws are the same men who employ the services Josh Barnes provides. Do you think they'd ever turn on him? Their reputations are at stake every time they have an encounter with one of Josh's girls. If we ever told, I'm afraid even if he didn't kill us, one of them would be sure to have it done. Powerful men like them aren't about to lose everything because of us. You can't trust anyone. Not even the police."

"There are more decent cops than bad."

"Say you do find one you think you can trust. What do you think will happen the minute word goes through the precinct? I'd lay odds that the cop would meet with a tragic end."

Blaine appeared to let her words sink in. "How can you stand sleeping with those men every night, Kami? Have you become so hardened that it doesn't bother you in the least?"

Kami's eyes grew cold and bitter. "I try not to think about them. I close my eyes and imagine I'm with someone I truly love. In time, you'll get used to it. I know you don't believe me now, but after a while it becomes monotonous and mechanical." Her lips grew taut. "Just keep your mind focused on the money," she tiredly replied. "That's all you can do. That's all there is."

"No, I won't. Not ever." She firmly set her jaw. "No one has the right to do this to us. There has to be someone we can trust."

"There's not. Welcome to your life, Blaine."

"You don't mean that." Blaine buried her face in her hands. "I can't do it," she sniffed. "Kami, I'm not even on birth control or anything!" she blurted out. "What if I get pregnant by one of them?" A shudder rippled through her.

Kami frowned. "I don't believe you, Blaine. What century are you living in?"

"I'm serious," she cried. "I've always wanted to wait until the right guy came along. The man I would hopefully spend the rest of my life with. Yes, I'm old-fashioned, but I've always believed that my virginity was the greatest gift I could give my husband on our wedding night."

Kami was silent for a moment. "You don't mean to tell me…" Her face registered the shock she felt. "Oh, Blaine! Josh was the first, wasn't he?"

Blaine nodded as tears rolled down her cheeks.

"Wait until Josh hears this! We've got to get you some

birth control. He never had you checked out."

"What do you mean checked out?"

"All the girls are medically examined from head to toe. But then, those girls have been around the block and even though some of them want out after they're in, they all came to Josh on their own."

"He's never forced anyone before?"

"No." Kami trembled as she looked at Blaine. "I'm so sorry, Blaine. I know that no matter what I say you won't believe me, but I am sorry. I'll try to help you, but please do what I say for now. You've got to promise me that you won't say or do anything to make Josh suspect. I'll figure out something."

"I promise," she whispered.

"First thing we have to do is get those detectives off your back. Tomorrow morning call them and tell them you'll come down to the station. That's all they want. If you don't they'll keep hounding you until you do."

Blaine's eyes widened. "What will Josh say?"

She shrugged. "Nothing. He said we should get rid of them. The quicker you do it, the quicker they'll get out of our lives for good. He'll understand that."

****

Jane studied her partner carefully. Casey looked good in her jeans and brown sweater, but then she had the figure and natural beauty that seemed to look good no matter whether her attire was, casual or dress. Her auburn hair glistened in the precinct's harsh light. She was much prettier than she gave herself credit for. She kept her trim figure by regularly working out in a gym and jogging whenever she could find the time. "You know what you need, Casey? You need to get out more. Socialize. Have some fun and enjoy life."

"I do enjoy life," Casey absently answered as she scanned a report.

Jane scowled. "No, you don't. You're always working. When was the last time you had a date or went out for a night on the town? You put in more overtime than anyone in the station." She leaned toward her. "What about Harry? He really liked you. What happened to him?"

"I'm happy and fulfilled in my life at the moment, Jane. Why do you bring the same topic up every other day? First, you were fixated on my relationship with Greg. Now it's Harry." Casey threw her pencil down as she rolled her big brown eyes. "For your information, Harry is a mama's boy. He wants someone to take care of him like Mommy does. The man drove me crazy! All he ever talked about was his mother. I swear to God, Harry couldn't even get through a meal without calling home every twenty minutes. I pity any woman who ends up with him. All I can say is they'd better have a bed big enough for the three of them."

Jane laughed. "Come on, he wasn't that bad. At least he's good-looking. He's got that going for him."

"He loses the minute he starts talking about Mommy." She grinned. "And for your unasked question, there's always Greg when I feel the urge."

"Casey! I wasn't even thinking that."

She grinned. "Jane, believe me when I say that I'm happy and content with the single life. I'm a complete woman and I have no complaints. I don't need a ring on my finger or a man by my side to feel whole."

"Maybe you'll change your mind once you meet the right man." Jane's eyes narrowed. "Stan's got this friend —"

"So good for Stan," she broke in.

"How about coming to dinner tomorrow night?"

71

"Can't."

"And why not?"

"I've got plans."

"I'll expect you at seven. That's an order!" Jane smiled. "Now, are you ready to give me a ride home?"

"Sure. Give me a minute."

Jane walked over to Casey's desk and leaned over her shoulder. "You'll never change, Casey."

"God help us if I do."

****

Later Casey curled up on her sofa and sipped at her cup of tea. She couldn't get Blaine Kirsten out of her mind. When she and Jane had tailed Josh Barnes to an exclusive condo, they watched as he sauntered inside. He turned once and Casey was certain he saw her. She noted how he carried himself with a smug confidence. His arrogance fitted his dress. He was extremely good-looking, and it was clear that he knew it and used it to his advantage. She decided to run a check on him. She was worried about Blaine. The kid was scared and trying to reach out to Casey or why else would she have called? She picked up her cell phone and pressed Jane's number. She waited a few seconds.

Jane's groggy voice finally came over the line. "What is it, Casey?"

"Jane, I was just sitting here thinking about Blaine. Do you think it would be wise for me to call her? We haven't touched base with her since the other afternoon when Kami Matthews interrupted the phone call."

Jane yawned. "Okay. We can call her in the morning. If Kami Matthews interrupts again, we'll go over there. Now get some sleep. Good night."

****

72

Casey paced around her large living room, admiring her antique rocker and other antiques, which had taken her years to acquire. Her contentment only came from her material possessions. Most of her friends, and especially Jane, assumed she needed a man to fill a void in her life. They couldn't understand that the void she felt went much deeper. She needed to find family — that was her missing link. Jane always tried to include her in family activities to make her feel as though she were part of Jane's own family, but the point was Casey knew she wasn't really a part of any family and it deeply disturbed her.

She craved someone who was of her own flesh and blood and to talk about the family history she remembered her parents sharing with her. She yearned for the baby sister who had been as abruptly snatched from her life as her parents had been. Through the years, she'd learned how precious and sacred every moment was with those you loved and cared about. She vowed that when she found her sister, they would strengthen the bond between them, the bond she'd never given up on. She knew only too well how quickly someone you loved could disappear from your life in the blink of an eye.

She walked into the bathroom and studied her reflection in the floor-length mirror. Her facial features were above average, with her brown eyes spaced perfectly. Her cheekbones were high and her skin was baby-soft and vibrant. She pinned her hair back and massaged cold cream into her face as she tried to chase her disturbing thoughts of Blaine from her mind. Blaine's bruised body had almost caused Casey to scoop the young woman into her arms and let her know that she no longer had to fear the demons. She had someone who cared about what happened to her, someone who'd always cared through the long dark years. She wondered what Blaine's reaction would be when she learned that Casey was her sister.

Chapter Six

"Casey, there's a Blaine Kirsten here to see you. She's in the conference room," a young officer said peering at her.

Casey set her pen down. "Thanks, Joe." She looked quizzically at Jane. "Looks like she's saved me a call. This may just be our lucky day."

"Let's find out."

Blaine turned when the detectives entered the room. "I've come to make the identification and sign the statement," she said. "I'm ready to put that creep behind bars for a long time."

Casey grinned. "Great!"

"I'll go get everything set up," Jane replied.

"How've you been?" Casey softly asked after Jane left the room. She quickly gave her the once over, relieved that no new bruises were evident.

"Fine, thanks." Blaine fidgeted with the clasp on her purse.

"Can I get you some coffee or tea?"

"Okay, coffee would be fine." She smiled shyly. "It's getting cold outside." She rubbed her hands together.

"Yes, and it's always chilly in this room." She filled two disposable cups. "Here you go. I don't know how good it is.

Jane made it." She laughed then made a face.

"Did I hear my name mentioned?" Jane asked walking back into the room.

"I was just telling Blaine that you made the coffee." She winked at Blaine. "Drinker beware!" She winked again. "Jane's coffee is great for those long work nights when you need something to keep you awake or if you suddenly find the need to pave a road. Usually thick as tar."

Blaine giggled. Casey noticed how beautiful the young woman was when she relaxed and let her guard down. She had a fragile, almost delicate air about her. The previous tough sarcasm she had exhibited toward them was an act she used to protect herself with, but when one chipped away the brick wall she placed around herself a charming human being was found.

"Thanks a lot, partner. By the way, Blaine, I at least passed my home economics course in high school," Jane said with a smile.

"I usually use instant myself," Blaine said and laughed. "Home Ec was the only class I ever flunked.

"Whew! Glad I wasn't the only one. Well, I suppose we'd better get down to business. We're going to walk down the hall for a minute to another room and several men will be brought in. I want you to look them over carefully and see if your attacker is in the lineup. If you see him tell me his number."

"Will he see me?" Blaine trembled as she looked at Casey.

"No. You'll be able to see him through the glass, but he can't see you."

Twenty minutes later they were back in the conference room. "Here's the statement." Jane laid it on the table. "Why don't we all sit down and go over it?"

"What happens after I sign this?" Blaine asked as she removed her coat. "I already identified him."

"The statement is what you told us about the attack." Casey wondered if the high turtleneck sweater Blaine wore was to hide her bruises. It certainly wasn't cold enough to warrant such a heavy sweater and overcoat. "You'll be called to testify in court," she answered. "That is unless he pleads guilty. In that case, you won't have to do anything."

Blaine hesitated. "I don't know about testifying," she said quietly.

"It's the only way. If you don't, he'll be back out on the streets." Casey stared hard at her. "Without your testimony, the prosecutor will have a very weak case. You don't want to give him the opportunity to get away with it and do it again, do you?"

Blaine nervously looked from one detective to the other. "There's no other way?"

"None," Casey answered as Jane shook her head. "But he might plead guilty. Many times they do."

She sighed. "I guess I'll have to do it then." She signed the statement and slid the paper back to Jane. "Is that all I need to do?"

"That's it. We'll be in touch with the status of the case." Casey smiled.

"Blaine, can you tell us what's been going on with you?" Jane asked.

Casey looked at Jane in surprise. She wasn't sorry that Jane had asked, though. She looked at Blaine to gauge her reaction to Jane's question.

Blaine trembled as she took a sip of her fresh cup of coffee. "I don't know what you mean," she answered. Her eyes were focused on the marred table.

Casey laid a hand on Blaine's arm. "You called me for help the other day. Then Kami Matthews took the phone from you. Are you afraid of her for some reason?" she asked gently.

Blaine's eyes brimmed with tears. She helplessly looked at Casey.

"What's wrong, Blaine?" Casey asked. "We can help you no matter what you tell us."

Blaine blinked hard choking back sobs.

"What are you afraid of?" Jane gently prodded. "Tell us about the accident you said you were in. What happened?"

"I can't talk about it," she cried, her heavy eyelids fluttering as her tears began to spill over.

"Why?"

"I…I can't."

"Are you afraid of Kami? Is that it, Blaine?" Casey persisted hating the haunted look that appeared in Blaine's red-swollen eyes. "Is that who you're afraid of?"

She sniffed. "No. Kami's as scared as I am." She drew a shaky breath. "She puts on a big act around you because she knows there's nothing we can do…there's nothing anyone can do."

"You've lost me. Can you explain what you mean?" Casey asked as she toyed with her coffee cup.

"No." Tears slid down her cheeks. "Please don't ask me to. I've already said too much."

Casey became frustrated. There had to be a way to get Blaine to open up. Blaine wanted their help, but only seemed able to accept it if they figured out what she was so afraid of. Maybe that was her way of protecting herself. If they figured it out, it would be okay, but not for her to come right out and tell them. She decided to dig the information out of Blaine if that's what it took. She'd play the game and Blaine would feel reassured that she didn't just spill her guts, but only answered the questions put to her. "Who was that man at Kami Matthews' apartment last night? The good-looking one. He's quite a sharp dresser." She had no clue whether he was visiting Kami's apartment or another one, but Blaine didn't know that.

Her breath caught in her throat. "I don't know who you're talking about," she said haltingly as she reached for her coat. "I have to go now." She quickly stood up, spilling the coffee. "I'm sorry," she cried. "I can't say any more. I've said too much as it is."

Casey sighed. So much for digging the information out of her, she thought. She watched Blaine closely. But at least she now knew that somehow Barnes was connected. But how? His record had come back clean so any hope of collaring him for an outstanding arrest warrant was unlikely.

Jane grabbed her arm. "Come on, Blaine. What's going on? Drugs? You can't fool us. We know you weren't in any accident. Who beat you up? Who are you afraid of? We're on your side! You don't deserve this and whoever did this to you needs to be locked up!"

Blaine looked at the detectives. Her body trembled, and she fought back fresh tears as she threw herself into Jane's arms, finally releasing all the pain and fear that had been holding her captive.

Casey nodded at Jane. "Blaine," she said. "Please trust us. We won't let you down. Come sit back down. Talk to us. Please," she pleaded. "If it's protection you need we'll provide it. There are many services at your disposal. All you have to do is ask."

Blaine swiped at her eyes as she reseated herself.

"You've got to promise me that this is just between us." She sniffed. "You can't mention a word of this conversation to anyone, not even Kami."

"We promise," Casey answered.

Blaine took a long shuddering breath. "You're right. I wasn't in an accident. I was beaten," she answered slowly, her face contorting in agony at the memory. "I knew you'd think it odd that I could be attacked twice just days apart by two different men. I'm not defending Kami, but she didn't really mean to get me involved. She had no choice. I know that now. She tries to act like it doesn't bother her, but it does. I've known her for far too long. I can see through her act."

Casey's jaw tightened as she gripped the edge of the table. No one had a right to physically abuse anyone, but when she saw on a daily basis women beaten by their husbands and lovers, or the prostitutes beaten and abused by their johns, it was sometimes more than she could bear. She tried to understand the victims' fear of retaliation and revenge and knew that was what kept so many of them from testifying. She didn't know what she herself would do in their place. Some of those who were brave enough to put their fears aside and testify later were murdered or beaten almost beyond recognition for trying to put an end to the abuse. It was a touchy topic, but she knew she'd risk her own life to protect Blaine.

"Start from the beginning," Jane urged in a sympathetic motherly tone of voice. "Take your time, Blaine."

Blaine cleared her throat. "I didn't know why Kami was so insistent that I stay at her apartment with her until the other night. Then it became clear that Josh's plan could only be implemented once I was there."

"I thought it was a good idea for you to stay at Kami

Matthews' apartment when she suggested it the morning I interviewed you at your apartment," Casey said. "What happened to you in her apartment?"

Blaine's eyes grew wild with fear. "No, you don't understand."

"What don't we understand, Blaine?" Casey leaned in closer.

"I was set up. It was already planned that I would be moving in with Kami. It hadn't mattered whether that creep had attacked me or not the other night. It just made the plan easier for Kami to carry out. One way or the other I would be moving into that apartment."

"Wait a minute," Jane broke in. "I thought Kami was your friend."

"She is and I felt betrayed by her until I found out why she lured me into the trap. She never wanted to and she tried to stall for time, but Josh wouldn't give her any more time."

Casey frowned. "Blaine, this isn't making any sense. What happened the other night? What did Barnes do to you?"

Her eyes painfully shifted. She drew a shuddering breath. "I was beaten and raped," she said in a barely audible voice.

Casey's eyes narrowed. "Was it Barnes?" she demanded.

She took another ragged breath. "Yes, Josh Barnes beat and raped me." Her voice broke into heart-wrenching sobs.

Casey's face flushed with anger as she saw the humiliation wash over Blaine with every tear that slid from her eyes. "That bastard!" She slammed her fist down on the table. "Level with us, Blaine. Why didn't you turn him in? What's going on?" Her eyes brimmed with tears of rage.

"Calm down," Jane warned her. "Don't let your

emotions take over," she whispered out of Blaine's earshot.

Casey put her head in her hands. "I'll be all right." She took a deep breath. "Okay. Tell us everything you know. Start at the beginning because, frankly, none of this is making any sense."

Blaine's eyes flitted nervously. "You can't say anything. He'll kill us!"

"No one is going to harm you or Kami Matthews. We'll protect you." Casey stared into Blaine's frightened eyes. "Please, Blaine, tell us what's going on."

Blaine wiped at her eyes with the tissue Jane offered. "The night I moved in with Kami, Josh Barnes came over. I thought he was a friend of hers, someone she was dating. I told her that I'd stay out of their way to give them some privacy, but she insisted that I meet him." Fresh tears rolled down her cheeks. "Josh kept saying these terrible things to me and touching me all over my body." She shuddered. "Kami told him that I didn't know yet." She blew her nose.

"What happened then?" Jane's voice was low.

"He became upset and started yelling and then he pushed Kami to the floor. I tried to run for help, but he grabbed me before I could and dragged me into the bedroom. I tried to fight him off, but he kept hitting me." She swallowed hard. "He made me do some of the most perverted things to him and he…" her voice trailed off. With a shaky hand, she dabbed at her eyes, and then blew her nose again. "Later after he'd gone, I told Kami that I was going to call the police, but she said I couldn't because I was one of Josh's girls now," she cried. "The other night Josh brought two men over. Kami took one of them into the bedroom." She hesitated. "And Josh forced me to have sex with the other one. It made me sick! I didn't want to do it, but I have no choice now. He owns me!

Don't you see?" she sobbed, looking at the two detectives. "I feel so cheap, so worthless now."

Casey's stomach muscles constricted. She struggled to keep her composure as she looked at Jane. "What do you think?" she asked in an uneven voice.

"Did you see any money being exchanged between the men and Barnes?" Jane questioned.

"No, but Josh gave Kami some money and he tried to give me some, but I wouldn't take it. I threw it in his face."

Casey leaned close to Blaine. "If we promise to protect you—"

"No!" Her voice rose shrilly. "You can't! He'll kill us! Kami says he has connections! You promised me you wouldn't say anything to anyone if I told you! Please!"

"Calm down, Blaine. We'll figure something out. Do you still have my cell phone number?" Casey asked.

"No. Kami tore it up. She said it was better that way."

She rolled her eyes. "Some friend."

"She's only doing what she thinks is right," Blaine said defensively.

Casey sighed, disliking Kami Matthews even more than she already did. "All right." She scribbled her number on a card. "Here. Keep this in a safe place. Whatever you do, don't let Kami know you have it. If you need me, please call."

"I will." She smiled weakly at Casey and Jane, and then stared down at her hands. "I want to tell you something else."

"What?" Casey asked.

"I just want you to know this." She cleared her throat. "It's difficult for me to talk about all of this. I...I was a virgin when Josh Barnes raped me." She clasped her hands tightly as her eyes lowered to her lap. "It was the most degrading moment of my life when he..." She didn't complete the thought.

Casey's eyes once again filled with tears. She opened her mouth to speak, and then suddenly changed her mind. There were no words to properly express her emotions with Blaine's revelation. Her stomach churned sickening her even further. She'd get the bastard! She was certain of it. The cocky son of a bitch would get his. Her heart rapidly thumped as she looked once again into Blaine's terror-stricken face. Barnes was a dead man. His days were numbered.

Chapter Seven

Casey allowed her mind to wander, eagerly hoping for an early end to this evening. She wasn't in a sociable mood and had tried every excuse imaginable to try to get out of this dinner, but Jane wouldn't hear of it. Casey wanted to be alone. She needed to think. Her head pounded as she recalled Blaine's confession. She'd wanted to tell her then and there that they were sisters. But it wasn't the right time. Now she wondered when the right time would come.

"Have some more wine, Casey," Jane offered.

Casey looked absently at her. "What? I'm sorry. What did you say, Jane?"

Jane laughed. "Loosen up. All work and no play makes Casey a very dull girl." She patted her husband's arm. "If you don't eat your chicken, Stan will think you don't like his choice of takeout," she teased. "And you know how he prides himself on his culinary abilities to order fast food."

Stan Adams chuckled as he looked up from his plate. "I'm sorry Jim had to cancel at the last minute, Casey." He leaned his solid frame back in his chair. "He had to see a client. It was a sudden thing that came up and he did try to get out of it. He's looking forward to meeting you, though, and I assured him that we'd set something up very soon."

85

Casey pushed her plate aside. "I wouldn't have been good company tonight anyway, Stan. It's been an exhausting day." She took her cigarettes from her purse.

Stan eyed her warily. "We don't allow smoking in our home, Casey. You know that. Besides, I thought you gave those up."

Casey put her cigarettes back into her purse. "Sorry. I did until a few days ago." She propped her elbows on the table and leaned her head against her hand. "It really is for the best that your friend canceled tonight, Stan. I'm afraid I would have made a horrible first impression. I'm too distracted to make any intelligent conversation."

"What's wrong, Casey?" he asked. "You haven't been yourself all night. Are you coming down with something? There's a stomach virus going around. It's pretty nasty from what I hear. A couple of guys I work with said their kids came down with it."

She sighed. "I wish it was the stomach flu."

Jane threw her napkin down. "I'll tell you what it is, Stanley. She's letting her emotions get in the way of her work." She frowned. "You've got to let it go or it'll destroy you, Casey," she cautioned. "Besides, we've had cases like this one before. What makes this one so personal for you?"

"I'll clear the table if you two want to talk," Stan offered.

Casey shook her head. "I can't talk about it right now," she said. "If you two don't mind, I think I'll call it a night." She rose. "I've got something to take care of."

"Is there anything I can do for you?" Stan asked with a tinge of worry in his voice. "Sometimes talking things out helps."

"I told you, Stan, that she's getting emotionally involved with a case we're working on."

Stan looked at his wife. "What is it?" he asked. "Someone you know, Casey?"

Jane eyed Casey carefully.

"It's complicated, Stan. It's a rape case," Casey wearily answered. "Actually, it's more involved than that."

"I thought that creep was behind bars." He propped his elbows on the table. "Did he get out on a technicality or something?"

"No. He is in custody. Casey's upset about another case." Jane grabbed Casey's arm. "Leave it alone, Casey. You can't do anything about it. She's got to ask us for help when she's ready. We can't force her. I think she told us more than she intended to."

"I know that, Jane, but the kid is trapped. We didn't force her to spill her guts. I think the only reason she did was because she believes we'll take it from there and help her. We told her we would. Remember? We have to help her. If we don't, who will? She's begging us to help her even though consciously she can't admit it."

Jane rubbed her forehead. "You heard what she said, Casey. If that bastard finds out that she talked to us, she's dead. Is that what you want? We can't protect her from him."

Casey raised her eyebrows. "Of course I don't want anything to happen to her, but the longer we wait, the more women get victimized, and the more money he makes off them."

"Our hands are tied right now," Jane insisted. "It's not a reported crime. If it were then that would be a different matter."

Casey's eyes flashed. "Why? We're cops and our job is to protect. We know what's going on and we're not doing anything about it. We're allowing this man to run a prostitution ring! He's forcing innocent young women into his operation."

"We have no concrete proof he's running anything. Think about it for a minute. What do you think those girls will say if we talk to them? We can't prove anything. They'll probably deny any wrongdoing. From what we observed, it appears they are living in the lap of luxury and I doubt they'll want to give that up. It's not like they're being forced into human trafficking. These women apparently can come and go as they please. They aren't being held against their will." Jane paused before continuing. "We can't force someone to file charges against her wishes. You know that, and the more we badger her the more she'll only pull away from us."

"Dammit, Jane! You saw how she broke down. She's terrified of what he'll do to her."

"And we offered her protection if she filed charges against him, but she turned us down flat."

"Come on, Jane. What do you expect her to do? How can you just sit there so nonchalantly and close off your mind to an innocent young woman's obvious suffering and cry for help?" she demanded heatedly. "She cried like a baby in your arms."

"Calm down, ladies," Stan said eying them cautiously. He ran a hand through his hair. "You're both getting a little hot under the collar. Can't you two discuss this calmly and rationally?"

Casey ignored Stan's comments. "What if it were your daughter, Jane? You and Stan are going to be starting a family soon. Think about it. If your own kid came to you with this story, what would you do?" Her face flushed. "Would you ignore her cry for help? Would you just walk away from her and tell her that there's really nothing you can do?"

"Casey, this is not my daughter. I can't help her!" Jane

shouted. "Your implication is totally unwarranted and unfair. If I could help this woman I would, but I can't until she's ready to help herself."

"A good cop will go the extra mile to help someone." Casey's eyes narrowed. "What side are you on, Jane?"

Jane sat in disbelief shaking her head back and forth. "I can't believe you would say that to me, Casey."

Casey ignored the hurt in Jane's eyes. "I never knew how cold and heartless you really are!"

Stan's eyes darkened. "That's enough, Casey! I don't know what your problem is, but I won't allow you to talk to my wife like this. She's a damned good cop and you know it!"

"I don't know what I know anymore." She slung her purse over her arm. "I'm out of here."

Tears stung Jane's eyes as she watched Casey walk out of the dining room. She quickly stood up knocking her chair over.

"Let her go, honey," Stan said. "I can't believe what she said to you."

"No, Stan. Something's wrong. I've never seen her like this. She didn't mean it. I know her too well."

She caught up to Casey as Casey was opening the apartment door. She placed a firm hand on Casey's arm. "Where are you going?" she demanded.

Casey pulled free from her grip. "I don't know. I've got to think. My head is all screwed up," she choked.

"Let me buy you a drink." Jane's voice was calmer now. "Let's talk this out."

"No. I want to be alone. Something is coming down, and I've got to figure out what I'm going to do."

"Come on, Casey. Whatever's bothering you, we'll work it out together as friends and partners. It's more than this case, isn't it?" she asked. "Dammit, Casey, what's going on with you? Talk to me!"

"No, I can't." Casey looked into her eyes. "You won't understand. Not until it's over."

"Until what's over? Tell me why Blaine Kirsten is affecting you like this."

"I've got to go. I'll see you in the morning."

****

"Put this on, Blaine. I want to see how it looks on you." Josh Barnes threw some lingerie at her. "You'll be entertaining a very important client in an hour. I won't tolerate another outburst. Do I make myself clear?"

Blaine started to protest, but saw Josh's warning look. Her body couldn't take another beating, physical or otherwise. She went into the bedroom Kami had given her and took her time changing. She wiped the hot tears that spilled from her eyes as she put the teddy on. She blew her nose and wiped her eyes. She applied some makeup and walked back into the living room.

Josh whistled appreciatively. "You're a beautiful sex goddess." He walked over to her and pinned her hair on top of her head, then stood back to admire her. "Perfect. I almost wish Mr. Allen would cancel." He smacked his lips. "I might just hang around for a little midnight snack later." He brushed a hand across the back of her neck. "Now you be a good girl and make sure Mr. Allen has a good time tonight. He's paying for an extra hour with you." He kissed her lips and fondled her breasts. "Nice."

Blaine knew the reaction he expected his caresses would cause. Maybe another woman would react passionately to his caresses, but not her. He repulsed her and her repulsion toward him mounted each time she saw him. She wanted to spit in his vulgar face and scratch his eyes out. She was a human being for God's sake, and he'd stripped her of all her rights. How could she ever escape his private prison?

"What about it?" he hoarsely whispered. "Will you save some for me?"

She drew her lips tightly together but didn't speak.

He cocked an eye. "I know I was your first, Blaine. Kami told me and I feel very privileged and honored to have been the one to take your virginity."

"You bastard!" she vehemently spat out. "You feel honored to have raped me?" She cringed waiting for his fist to come smashing into her face.

Before he could react, they heard the key in the lock.

"Who will I be entertaining tonight, Josh?" Kami asked as she hurried into the room, her arms filled with grocery bags.

"I'm giving you the night off, my love," he answered good-naturedly as he took the packages from her.

Blaine was surprised how quickly his mood had changed. That terrified her even more. He was sadistic and loved playing mind games.

Kami looked hesitantly at Blaine. "In that case, I guess I'll catch a movie if it's all right with you, Josh."

"Yes, that sounds like a perfect idea. Why don't you run along now? I need to talk to Blaine privately before Mr. Allen arrives."

"Let me put the groceries away first."

"No. I'll take care of them."

Blaine tried to catch Kami's eye. She wasn't sure whether Kami acknowledged that fact or if she was deliberately avoiding eye contact with her.

"I'll change my clothes and then be out of here."

"Make it quick or I might change my mind."

Kami walked into her pale blue bedroom, pulled the drapes together, then sat on the edge of her bed. She picked up her large stuffed teddy bear and held it close to her chest. That stuffed toy had been with her since she was a child. They'd been through all of Kami's trials and tribulations together. She looked into the teddy bear's glass eyes and smiled. She set him back in his place on the pillows. How had she let her life get so out of control? She had no one to blame but herself. She despised herself for dragging Blaine into this mess. No matter how she tried to justify her actions, it came back to one fact. She was a coward. She'd put her own life before Blaine's. Even though Blaine seemed to ease up on her, she knew that nothing would be the same between them. She was worried about Blaine. She didn't want to leave her alone with Josh— something didn't feel right. A feeling of foreboding enveloped her. Blaine hated Josh and the more she resisted him, the more violent he would become. Kami had seen it before. It was a challenge to him and one where he always came out the victor. Blaine didn't stand a chance.

She gazed around her large bedroom with all its magnificent silks and satins and knew that it didn't mean anything to her anymore. She'd been ecstatic when Josh had rented this apartment, not knowing at the time that he had purchased the entire building, among others, and that the apartments were filled with his "girls". In the beginning, she was overwhelmed with money and the luxuries she received. But something had still evaded her. All the money in the world would never bring her happiness. This apartment now brought her only countless memories of shame and humiliation. She desperately wanted out. She craved a normal life where she could go on dates, have people over, and maybe even someday find someone special to share her life with. She had everything money could buy, but the price she'd had to pay was her freedom. She'd sold her own soul to the devil and the devil was Josh Barnes. She sighed dejectedly as she left the room, and then slowly walked down the carpeted hall toward the entrance, swallowing hard as she quietly let herself out of the apartment.

She'd wanted to say good-bye, but she couldn't bear looking into Blaine's haunted eyes any longer. She didn't expect Blaine to ever believe how truly sorry she was for dragging her into this, but she hoped that Blaine could see how what she had done tortured her soul and always would. She'd never meant to hurt Blaine. She'd always enjoyed the friendship they shared. That was the truth, but she was the only one who would ever know it now. She was certain that Blaine would never believe her, even if she acted otherwise. It was an act since she now would become Kami's permanent roommate. Blaine would always assume that Kami had kept their friendship only because of Josh's orders. In Blaine's place, she knew that she would feel the same way. Betrayal was something one never got over.

****

Josh mixed two drinks, handed one to Blaine, and then settled himself on the plush sofa, resting his boot-clad feet on the coffee table. "Come sit by me, baby." He patted the empty space next to him.

"No, thank you." Blaine avoided eye contact with him as she fidgeted with a silky tie on her teddy.

"Come on. You know how impatient I am." His eyes slanted. "Now!"

She slowly walked across the room, and then stiffly seated herself next to him.

He ran his fingertips down her arm. "Lighten up, Blaine. I don't bite. You should know that by now." He laughed sarcastically. "Come on, don't treat me so cold, baby. After all, it's not like we've never been intimate. A little more time and you'll be so hot in bed that these guys will fight to be with you." He touched her hair. "Or is it the emotional attachment because I was your first?" He pulled her close as his lips hungrily sought hers.

She placed her hands on his chest pushing away from him. "Don't! I'll be all messed up when Mr. Allen gets here."

He reluctantly released her. "You're right." He sipped at his drink. "I've got to talk to you anyway."

She looked up at him. "What?" His dark eyes penetrated hers. She could almost feel the fire in them searing her flesh.

"Why are you so chummy with those two detectives?" He swirled the glass in his hand and the ice cubes tinkled against one another. He continued to stare at her as he waited for her answer.

Her breath caught momentarily in her throat. "What do you mean?" she asked innocently.

His eyes narrowed. "Don't play dumb with me."

"I'm not, Josh." She tried to mask her nervousness, but her hand trembled.

He laid a heavy hand on her arm. "I want the truth," he demanded. His fingers dug into her flesh. "They tailed me the other night and I want to know why! What did you tell them?"

She winced. "I don't know why they did that. They just wanted to talk to me about the guy who attacked me. You know all about that. I didn't tell them anything else."

"I'm going to be watching you very closely, honey, so you'd better be leveling with me." He released her arm.

"I am." She rubbed her arm.

"You know what will happen if you're lying to me." He looked at her for a long minute. "Don't forget what I said."

The familiar gentle tapping on the door finally broke his gaze. He got up and sauntered over to the door.

Blaine heard muffled voices in the entrance hall. Seconds later Josh called her name. She joined the two men.

"Blaine, I'd like you to meet Dana Allen." He winked at Mr. Allen. "She's a little shy, but give her a chance and you won't be disappointed."

Blaine gave Dana Allen the once-over. He was short, stocky, and balding. The sight of him repulsed her. No way would she go to bed with this disgusting old man. Her insides viciously churned. She wanted to vomit. She gulped hard forcing the bile back down her throat.

"I'll let you two get better acquainted," Josh said leading them to the living room. He flicked on the television and seated himself back on the sofa. "After tonight, Dana, I guarantee that you'll want Blaine for your number one girl. I haven't been wrong yet."

Blaine's legs were shaking as she led the man to her bedroom. She closed the door, and then turned to him. "What…what do you want?" She sharply inhaled as she sat on the edge of the king-sized bed.

He touched her arm gently. "You're very new at this, aren't you?" he softly asked.

She blinked back tears. "Yes." Her voice shook.

He looked intently at her. "Why are you doing this? You're not like the other girls. I can see it in your eyes." He moved closer to her. She stiffened. "You don't want to do this, do you? I don't mean just tonight. You don't want to do this at all, do you?"

She longed to pour out to him what she was truly feeling and the sickness that was eating through her, but the words caught in her throat. "I—" She looked into his kindly, fatherly face. No, she couldn't. He was here for one thing and one thing only. If she didn't pull herself together and force herself to do it, he'd tell Josh. She drew a deep breath. "What do you like?"

Dana Allen continued to look at her. He did not attempt to remove his clothes. Instead, he moved to the bed and sat down next to her. "Look," he began. "I'm not going to make you go through with this." His voice was gentle and soothing. "I'm not going to force myself on you."

She looked skeptically at him. "Just tell me what you'd like me to do."

He frowned. "I have a daughter about your age." His eyes met hers. "I don't know what I'd do if she was entertaining men old enough to be her father or grandfather for money. Get out of this racket, Blaine. You're not the type who can survive in this kind of world."

"I have no choice."

"What do you mean?" he asked gently. "The women who work for Josh are here because they want to be. He carefully vets them for his and his clients' protection." His forehead furrowed. "Are you telling me that you are being forced into this?"

Blaine's lips trembled. How could she ever get out of this? How could she save other defenseless women from the same fate? He would continue his operation and there was no hope for the law to come down on him since his connections would make sure he was well protected.

"It'll be all right, Blaine." He shook his head. How about if I tell Josh that I've changed my mind."

"No! You can't. He expects me to do this!" she cried. "If not you then he'll just choose another client for me to, as he calls it, entertain."

"Are you afraid of him?" Dana asked. "Has he harmed you?" He looked closely at her. "Never mind. Your eyes speak volumes, Blaine."

Her eyes shifted nervously.

He gave her a fatherly hug. "Don't worry. He'll get his money and I promise not to tell him anything." He slowly shook his head back and forth. "I know you find it hard to trust me, but you can." He cleared his throat. "Looking at you, Blaine, makes me disgusted with myself. Men like me give Josh Barnes the opportunity to exploit young women like you. A man my age, and with my looks, can't attract a young beauty, so I buy them. I'm so sorry, Blaine. For the first time in a long time you've opened my eyes to what kind of man I really am."

Blaine looked at Dana Allen. Tears filled his eyes and she knew he was speaking from his heart. She knew she could really trust him. Suddenly she was overwhelmed with compassion for this man who just a few minutes before was ready to take her body for a price. "Thank you, Mr. Allen," she whispered. "Thank you."

He sighed heavily. "Don't thank me, Blaine. I'm just as guilty as Barnes is. Remember what I said, if it weren't for men like me, he'd be out of business. We demand and he supplies." He lit a cigar, and then smiled at her. "We've got twenty minutes to kill. How about a game of cards?"

She returned his smile, thankful for the reprieve—at least the reprieve for this night.

****

Jane sat at her desk sipping at a steaming mug of coffee.

She looked up when Casey approached her. "Good morning, Casey," she said. When Casey didn't respond, Jane looked sharply at her. Casey stood by her desk and leafed through her messages. "Where were you last night? You had me worried sick. Your cell phone went to voice mail. Did you turn it off? I figured if you did, you'd at least answer your home phone. I called your apartment all night long and all I got was that damned machine of yours. Why didn't you return any of my calls? How do you know it wasn't an emergency?"

Casey looked up. Her eyes met Jane's. "I wanted to be alone." She sat at her desk and picked up a folder.

Jane sat staring at her. Casey's attitude toward Blaine Kirsten frightened her. Casey was a good cop and never before had she allowed a case to dominate her emotions this way. There was more to it. She kept her eyes focused on Casey. Casey pretended to concentrate on the folder clutched in her hands, but Jane instinctively knew that her mind was elsewhere. There was a pained loneliness reflected in her eyes. Jane wished she could see what was going through Casey's mind. She would give anything to relieve her suffering, but Casey had shut her out and locked herself safely inside.

Jane's phone buzzed and she picked it up.

"We'll let her know." She put the phone down. "Casey, do you want to call Blaine and let her know that her stolen items are available for pickup?" She smiled. "That should make her happy."

Casey threw the folder down. "Okay." She picked up her phone and punched in the number. "Yes, Miss Matthews, this is Detective Jorgan. Would you please tell Blaine that she can come down to the station to pick up her items? Thanks." Casey put the phone down, and then looked at Jane. "What?" she asked.

"What was that all about?"

Casey raised her eyebrows. "I gave the message to Kami Matthews. She promised to relay it to Blaine."

"Why didn't you talk to Blaine yourself?"

"What for?" Her jaw was set stiffly as she picked up the folder again. "Matthews is capable of giving her the message."

"What's wrong with you, Casey?" Jane asked louder than she'd intended, then lowered her voice when she saw some of the other detectives looking curiously in their direction. "What's going on with you anyway?" she hissed. "And don't tell me nothing."

"Drop it, Jane. Remember that *you* started this."

"Started what?" When Casey didn't respond, Jane stood up. "I've got to see Officer Krespeck. We'll discuss this later."

"There's nothing to discuss."

****

Blaine pushed her hair from her brow. "I'm glad I was able to pick my things up. I wanted to take a minute to thank you."

Casey smiled. "Since you've come by to see us, I'd like to talk to you about something, Blaine, if you have the time."

She raised her eyebrows. "Okay."

Jane looked at Casey with a puzzled expression on her face.

"Let's go to the conference room so we can talk privately." Casey rose.

After they were seated around the conference table, Casey turned to Blaine. "I want you to help me put Barnes away for good. I know we can do it, but not without your help."

Blaine shook her head. "Count me out, Detective. I only came down here to pick up my things. I shouldn't have said anything the last time I was here. I'm not saying anything more about Josh Barnes. I told you before that he'd kill me and Kami." She twisted the hem of her jacket. "He's already warned me to stay away from you and Detective Adams. I told him I was only here to identify my attacker and sign a statement. If you keep contacting me, it's only making things worse for Kami and me."

"Look Blaine, this is our only chance to get him," Casey said.

"I'd like to help, but I can't. I'm sorry." She swallowed hard. "I'm in this now and that's a fact of my life. There's no way out. Kami was right about that. If there was, don't you think I'd take it?" Her lips trembled. She needed Casey to believe she would never have chosen this kind of life. She didn't know why Casey's opinion of her was so important, only that it was.

"Can't you see that this *is* your chance to get out?" Casey's eyes flashed angrily as she gripped the edge of the table so tightly that her knuckles turned white. "Isn't that what you want?"

Jane shot Casey a warning look. "Blaine, you don't have to do anything you're not comfortable with."

"What's the matter with you?" Casey rose, and then walked to where Blaine was seated. She stood staring hard at her for a full minute. "Maybe you like it, huh?" Her eyes flashed angrily. "That's it! You don't want our help because you enjoy the lifestyle. The money's finally gotten to you, hasn't it?"

"Detective Jorgan, that's enough!" Jane said.

Blaine stood up, facing Casey. "I...I—" Her voice quivered. "I thought you really cared!" she sobbed, running from the conference room.

"Sit down!" Jane demanded shoving Casey into a chair. "What the hell was that all about?" She wagged a finger under Casey's nose. "That was a stupid move! If you really want to help her, then that's a poor way of going about it. You treated her like a criminal! You know how she's suffered. How could you be so heartless and cruel?" Her eyes narrowed. "And you had the nerve to accuse me of being cold? What a laugh. Her case is closed. Accept it. Let her live her life. We have nothing on Josh Barnes."

"Just shut up, Jane!" Casey shouted as she rubbed her throbbing temples. "Just shut the hell up!"

Chapter Eight

"What happened to you?" Kami asked with a concerned look on her face.

Tears sprang to Blaine's eyes. "I went to the police station to pick up my things."

"I know, but what happened? You look upset."

She sank wearily into a chair, and then removed her shoes wriggling her cramped toes. "Detective Jorgan went ballistic on me. She's nuts!"

Kami cocked an eye. "Why? What happened? That doesn't sound like her. I mean, she appears a little rough in her questioning, but it doesn't make sense. I thought you were only picking up your things. Did you have to see her for some reason?"

"No, I thought I'd stop by and thank them for their help. You know, just to be nice."

"And?"

Blaine drew a deep breath. "I did something stupid." She looked at Kami. "I told them about Josh."

"You what!" Kami's face turned ashen. "Oh, God, Blaine. Why?"

"Not today. It was when I was making the identification and signing the statement. They were both so nice to me. I don't know...it just poured out. They were so caring and understanding then, but today Jorgan was a real bitch," she said bitterly. "She's pissed off because she wants to go after Josh and she wants me to help. She doesn't seem to care about the risk to you and me. All she cares about is making the bust to make herself look good. She actually accused me of liking to work for Josh." She bit her bottom lip. "She said some hateful things to me."

"What about Detective Adams?"

"She looked pissed off at Jorgan. I got out of there when Jorgan went off."

Kami let her breath out slowly. "Why did you mention Josh's name in the first place? They wouldn't have known anything if you'd just kept quiet." Her eyes flitted nervously back and forth. "What are we going to do?" She helplessly wrung her hands. "They'll tail him and he *will* find out about it."

"They must have already staked out the apartment because they knew Josh was here. I...I know what you said he'd do to us if we ever told," she stammered. "I didn't mean to tell them, Kami."

Kami grabbed her hands. "It's not your fault. Blaine, I know you'll never believe me, but I am sorry for all of this." Tears stung her eyes. "I don't expect you to ever forgive me, but please believe me when I say I really did try to protect you. I did everything in my power to convince Josh not to drag you into this."

"Kami," Blaine said in a low voice. "I know now that you had to do what Josh said. I don't blame you anymore since I've seen with my own eyes how cruel he really is. He never gives anyone a choice."

"Thank you," she whispered, swallowing the lump in

her throat. "You don't know what that means to me. You're the only true friend I've ever had."

"I feel the same way about you." Blaine smiled weakly. "I'm sorry I've risked your life by telling the cops about Josh. If anything happens to you I don't know how I'll live with myself." She was thoughtful for a moment. "But I probably wouldn't have to worry about it after Josh got done with me."

Kami rubbed her temples. "I'm so sick and tired of this life. Maybe you should help them, Blaine. This could be the break we both need. I know I can't do this for the rest of my life. And I definitely know you can't."

Blaine stared wide-eyed at her. "Didn't you hear a word I said? Jorgan accused me of enjoying being one of Josh's girls. She made me feel so cheap and dirty. She humiliated me. I'll never trust her now." She walked over to the well-stocked bar and poured herself a glass of wine. "She had no right to talk to me the way she did. How can I trust her to protect us now?"

"We don't have any choice, Blaine. I know I told you not to tell them anything, but I've been doing a lot of thinking lately and I really don't like the person I've become. I would do anything to have a normal life back. The grass really isn't any greener on the other side of the fence. I used to think money and material things were the answer to all my problems no matter how I got them. Now I would give anything to turn back time. But I can't." Her voice grew quiet. "I sacrificed everything for this." She spread her arms wide. "It's definitely not worth the price I have to pay."

"You had no choice either," Blaine replied. "So now you want me to help the cops?" She sipped her drink.

She nodded. "Yes. I don't think Detective Jorgan meant what she said. It's just her way of testing you."

"For what?" Blaine walked over to the window and

gazed out at the lively city below.

Kami joined her at the window. "She really cares about you, Blaine. She's putting on an act. There's more to it than she's letting on."

Blaine scowled. "What could possibly be her motive?"

Kami shrugged. "I don't know. Maybe she's close to someone who's been abused or something." She touched Blaine's shoulder. "Maybe I can figure out a way to get the both of us out of this mess and you won't have to do anything. At least I've got to try," she said softly. "And it certainly will help with the cops on our side. I'd rather have them with us than against us."

"Kami, you know he'll kill us! I can't let you do this! Look what he's already done to me. I don't think he'd even blink an eye if either or both of us turned up dead."

"I'll take the risk." She glanced at her watch. "I'm going to the station now. I'm telling Detectives Adams and Jorgan the whole story from beginning to end and how you were unwittingly dragged into it."

"I'm scared, Kami."

She gave her a friendly hug. "Keep calm," she whispered. "Everything will work out. You'll see. Before you know it, we'll be free from Josh. Maybe a little poorer, but our freedom means more than all the money in the world."

"Are you sure you want to do this?"

She nodded. "I should have done this a long time ago. I'm going now before I lose my courage. I may never get another chance."

****

Jane stood in front of Casey, feet slightly apart with hands on her hips. "Casey, I said I was sorry! Can you please just let it go now? We've got other cases we should be working on. We can't devote every waking minute to Blaine's case."

Casey glared at her. "You made a fool out of me in front of her!" She pointed her finger in Jane's face. "How could you do that to me? Don't you ever do that again!"

"I can't promise you that," Jane stated. "You were out of line. And I honestly hope that our friendship doesn't have to take a beating because of it. I think we are both too mature to let that happen."

"Just forget it, Jane. I can't talk to you right now."

"Well, you'd better start, partner. Look who just walked in."

Both women watched as Kami Matthews approached their desks stylishly dressed in a two-piece suit with matching jewelry. She held her head high as she neared their desks, then seconds later stood confidently before them.

"What can we do for you, Miss Matthews?" Casey asked in an even tone of voice.

"I need to talk to you. In private." She clutched her handbag tightly. "It's important!"

"About what?" Casey prodded.

"Blaine Kirsten."

Casey tensed.

Jane watched Casey's reaction and saw a dark shadow cross her face at the mention of Blaine's name. The shadow left Casey's face as quickly as it had come. Or was Casey just covering her emotions? What was really going on inside that head of hers? Jane wondered. She used to be able to read Casey like a book, but she didn't know what to think anymore. She wished she could figure out what it was about Blaine Kirsten that was driving her out of control.

Casey sat on the edge of her cluttered desk. "I'm sorry, Miss Matthews, but Blaine identified the suspect and we have no further need for her at the present time. She'll be notified when and if she's to appear in court to testify. Now if you'll excuse me, I have work to do." She picked up a folder and leafed through it, dismissing the young woman.

Jane's curiosity was piqued. "What about Blaine?" she asked.

"Could we talk somewhere in private, Detective Adams? Please?"

"We can talk here," Casey said.

Kami nervously looked around the busy room. "No. I'd feel better talking somewhere else."

"Okay. We can go to a conference room." Jane turned to Casey. "Are you coming, Detective Jorgan?"

"I'll be there in a minute," Casey replied, trying to regain her composure.

****

Blaine opened the door.

"Where's Kami?" Josh asked as he strode into the apartment. He removed his overcoat and handed it to her.

She was surprised to see him. She took his overcoat. "She had some errands to run, but she should be back soon." His casual attire surprised her. Usually he was dressed in a three-piece suit. Today he was dressed in jeans and a gray pullover.

"I thought I'd surprise her and take her on a special little trip for the weekend. She's been working extra hard lately." He chuckled. "If you know what I mean?" he added, with a wink.

Blaine ignored his insinuation. She hoped that Kami would return soon and with good news. She certainly wasn't in the mood to entertain this arrogant bastard.

"No need to worry, though. You'll still be watched just

in case you get any crazy ideas," he warned. "Fix me a drink, baby," he said, following her into the living room.

"The usual?"

"Of course."

She mixed the drink, and then handed it to him. Her hand slightly shook.

"You seem on edge," he said. "Something wrong?"

"No," Blaine replied forcing herself to calm down. "I'm just a little tired. That's all."

He smiled at her. "Mr. Allen was very impressed with you," he said as he seated himself in his usual position on the sofa.

"I'm happy to hear that." She would always be grateful to Dana Allen for keeping what really happened from Josh. Even though she wanted to trust the man, a part of her was still afraid he might tell Josh, especially if his reputation was at stake. She smiled politely, but inside she cringed.

"I knew from the first day I laid eyes on you that you were going to be hot stuff." He licked his lips. "Maybe you and I can have a little fun while I wait for Kami to return."

She grimaced. "I don't think so. Besides, I'm expecting someone," she lied. Her stomach muscles tightened. She couldn't bear the thought of his touching her again. He was contemptible. His hot hands ripping and clawing at her body disgusted her. She shuddered. She was forced to relive that horrible night in her mind every time she saw him. It ate away at her, suffocating her. If only Kami could get them out of this. She hoped the detectives would listen to her story.

"Who are you expecting?" he demanded. "No one comes in or out of this apartment without my approval."

"Just a friend." She avoided his eyes. She sat on the loveseat across from the sofa.

"You have no friends that I've been made aware of other than Kami." He eyed her coldly. "What's your friend's name?"

She didn't respond. She racked her brain trying to think of a name.

He set his drink on the coffee table, and then walked over to where she was sitting. "What are you up to? Who's really coming here? I know you're still seeing those detectives, aren't you?"

"I had to make a positive ID on the jerk that attacked me," she said in an even voice. "I've told you that repeatedly. That's the only connection I have with them. I haven't seen them since."

"That's not true. You made another visit to the police station. When you left you were crying."

"I had to pick up the things that were stolen from me during the attack."

"Okay, baby." He squeezed her arm threateningly. "Just remember my warning. If I find out you're lying to me, you won't like the consequences."

She knew he didn't believe her. "I'm telling you the truth," she nervously replied.

He eyed her suspiciously. "I don't know if I should trust you. Maybe you need a refresher course on who's in charge around here. What do you think?"

The look in his eyes terrified her. "You can trust me. I won't say anything — ever."

"You'd better start being a little nicer to me then." He moved closer. "Maybe you do need to be taught another lesson. You seem to forget who owns you." His eyes grew dark and his jaw tightened. "I don't want you talking to those detectives again."

"I won't."

He smirked at her. "I need to make sure that you won't."

"I promise I won't ever talk to them again. I'll do whatever you say, Josh," she pleaded.

He clamped his large hands on her shoulders and yanked her to her feet.

"I said I'd never tell," she cried. "Please don't hurt me, Josh," she whimpered.

With one hand, he swiftly ripped her blouse from her body and then grabbed her flimsy bra pulling it roughly off her. She winced as the material tore into her flesh. He leered at her exposed breasts. "Nice," he said. He took one in his hand and fondled it. He pinched the nipple.

"You're hurting me, Josh." She pushed his strong chest. "Get away from me!" She raised a knee and tried to kick him, but he quickly grabbed her leg. "You're sick!

His eyes grew wild. "What did you say?" He swung his arm back still holding onto her leg with his other hand, and then quickly brought it forward, hitting her in the mouth. The force of the blow sent her whirling backward as blood spurted from her mouth. She frantically grabbed at a table to get her balance and sent a lamp crashing to the floor. She tasted thick, salty blood in her mouth. He lunged at her, and she kicked and clawed at him. She was no match for his strength, but she continued punching, kicking, and clawing at him with every ounce of strength she could muster as he quickly overpowered her. "Help!" she screamed.

"Bitch!" he hissed. "Who do you think is going to hear you? You were warned." He brought his fist up again.

She lay in a heap on the floor. He straddled himself over her forcing her to straighten her body. She tried to free her arms, but he had them securely pinned at her sides with his strong legs. She recoiled as she watched his large fist descend as if in slow motion toward her face. She squeezed her eyes shut, as his fist came crashing into her face. Her face felt like it had been crushed in. She tasted her blood mixed with her vomit as Josh's face swam dizzyingly in front of her half-closed eyes. She was going to pass out. Or maybe she was dying. She didn't know.

He released her just enough to undo his jeans. "Tell me you want it, baby," he whispered hoarsely. "Tell me you need a real man to fuck you. Not those old fools I provide for you."

She tried to focus her eyes, but a sharp pain in her head and the nausea that followed made her close them. Bile continued to rise and gurgle in her throat almost choking her. She started to open her mouth, but the throbbing sent shockwaves through her body. Blood oozed out of the corner of her mouth.

He quickly tore the remaining clothes from her body. "Tell me you want it, hot stuff," he breathed into her ear. When she didn't respond, he grabbed her hair, yanking her head back so hard she thought her neck would snap. "Tell me!" he screamed.

She gasped choking and swallowing the hot bile that had crept into her mouth. "I...want...it," she answered in a strangled voice and then succumbed to the blackness that quickly surrounded her.

****

"Okay, Miss Matthews, what's on your mind?" Jane asked.

Kami laid her coat over the back of a chair. "Blaine told me that you want her to help you put Josh Barnes out of business."

111

Jane nodded. "That's correct. We asked for her cooperation."

"She turned us down," Casey added.

Kami cautiously eyed Casey. "I…I want to do it," she said quickly, before she could change her mind. "I'll tell you everything I know about him."

"You!" Casey retorted. "As I understand it, you got her into this in the first place. Now we're supposed to trust you?" She placed her hands on her hips. "How do we know this isn't a setup?"

Kami's eyes lowered. "I know I'm to blame for this whole mess Blaine is in, but I had no choice." Her eyes narrowed as she raised them and stared into Casey's penetrating eyes. "You don't know the whole story." Her lips trembled. "If you did then maybe you would feel differently about me instead of harboring such a harsh opinion of me."

"Why should we trust or believe anything you say?" Casey asked sarcastically. "Why don't you enlighten us about what's going on and we'll decide if we believe you or not?"

"Why don't you just get off my back, Detective Jorgan? I don't know why you don't like me since you know nothing about me, but personally, I don't care. Whatever it is that bothers you about me is your own problem, but you have no right to take it out on me. I'm here to help Blaine."

Casey's jaw tightened as she kept her eyes focused on Kami. "Take this friendly piece of advice, kid. You've got a smart mouth and it's going to be your downfall someday."

"Do you think for one minute that I really like myself?" she asked in a quivering voice. Her eyes glistened. "Because I don't!"

Casey snorted. "What am I supposed to do? Pity you while you live in the lap of luxury? Turn off the phony tears.

You'll get no sympathy from me."

Kami sniffed. "I don't want your sympathy. That's not what this is all about. If it makes you feel any better, I can't stand the person I've become! I can't stand what I did to Blaine. All I want to do is help her now. Can't you give me a break?" she cried. "I'm the scum of the earth—is that what you want to hear? Does it make you feel better? Yes, I am worthless!" she screamed as her body shook almost uncontrollably.

Casey paced back and forth across the worn floor for a few seconds before speaking. "I don't know, Miss Matthews. It still sounds to me like you're setting us up and maybe putting Blaine in further jeopardy. How do I know it's not just a ploy you and Barnes set up?"

"No, I'm not setting you or Blaine up. I swear! You've got to trust me. Please!" she pleaded. "I'll tell you everything I know about Josh Barnes." Her body shuddered. "I know you don't like me, Detective Jorgan, and I don't blame you, but I saw how concerned you were about Blaine the first day you met her. Do it for her!" she pleaded. "Just trust me now for Blaine's sake. I'll sign anything you want me to, to prove I'm not lying to you. I can give you client names. Anything you want, but for God's sake I have to save Blaine."

"Back up for just a minute, Miss Matthews. I am not treating Blaine any differently than I would any victim of a crime. I do not show favoritism or get emotionally involved with any case if that's what you are implying. If Blaine wants our help, she's been informed to contact us."

Kami swiped at her eyes with the back of her hand. "All right, then," she exhaled as she held her head high. "I'm sorry I wasted your time. I'll find some other way to help Blaine." She turned to Jane. "Thank you for your time, Detective Adams." She avoided looking at Casey. She grabbed her jacket and walked to the door. As she turned the knob she felt a warm hand cover her own. She looked up in surprise into the eyes of Detective Jorgan. Only now, the detective's eyes had lost the coldness and were filled with gentleness.

Jane's forehead furrowed at the abrupt change in Casey. The back and forth in her attitude was not normal, and Jane was still determined to get to the bottom of it. But for now, she needed to focus on Kami Matthews.

"Come on, kid." Casey's voice had softened. "Tell me everything you know." She led Kami back to the table.

"Thank you, Detective Jorgan." Kami seated herself.

"Would you like some coffee?"

"Thank you, yes."

"I'll go get you a cup," Casey replied while Jane walked to the table and seated herself across from Kami.

"Is Blaine all right?" Jane asked.

"For now, but I don't know how much longer she can go on."

"You won't change your mind about helping us?"

"I won't. I'll even sign a statement if I must to prove that you can trust me."

"No need," Jane said softly.

They both looked up when Casey opened the door, walked over to the table, and set a steaming cup of coffee in front of Kami.

Chapter Nine

Blaine struggled to pull herself to her feet, but fell back exhausted in a heap. She wondered how long she'd been out. The excruciating pain made her dizzy and she knew that at any moment she could black out again. Where was Josh? Had he gone? Her stomach felt like a knife had been plunged into it, and every breath she took seemed to push the knife even deeper inside. She dug her nails into the plush thick carpeting and turned on her side. The effort made her nauseous and she vomited. She struggled again to raise herself and this time managed to get to her knees. She tried for several seconds to raise her head. Finally, with sweat and blood dripping from her, she looked up.

Josh stood threateningly above her. His boot-clad feet were spaced slightly apart as he glared down at her. "Have you learned your lesson?" It was more of a statement than a question.

She was oblivious to her nakedness as she frantically tried to force herself to her feet. She clutched the leg of a chair and tried to pull herself up. Her body screamed with pain. She let go of the chair leg, and whimpering buried her face in the carpet. "Why?" she whispered in a raspy voice. "Why me?"

"Because, baby, you just won't give up. You keep fighting me, but the sooner you accept the fact that I own you, the better we'll get along. Now, are you going to start doing things my way?" He stooped down glowering at her. "I'm waiting for an answer."

She turned her face toward him. "No," she whispered through clenched teeth. "Never...you'll have to kill me first."

"That can be arranged." He stood up, and then backed away from her.

She squeezed her eyes shut as she moaned in pain. It was quiet. Maybe he'd gone. Please come back, Kami, she silently prayed. Just as she thought she was in the clear, without warning, his heavy boot came crashing down, striking her in the chest. Her lips parted and the foreboding black pit enveloped her.

****

"Detectives, could you please call me Kami?" Kami shyly asked. "You've always called Blaine by her first name." She didn't know why that fact bothered her, but it did. She wanted them to care about her well-being as much as it was apparent that they cared about Blaine's. She was tired of going through life without anyone being able to see the person she really was deep inside. She'd show them that she wasn't the monster they seemed to think she was, but instead a decent, honest, and sincere human being worthy of being cared about and protected.

Casey nodded. "No problem."

"Okay, Kami, why don't you start at the beginning and tell us everything," Jane said as she leaned back in a chair.

"It's a long story," she answered twisting her hands together.

"We've got time. Tell us how you got involved with

116

Josh Barnes," Casey prompted. "And how you met Blaine."

"Okay." She took a deep breath. "I grew up in a good middle-class family. I knew Blaine from school." She watched Casey's eyes brighten at the mention of Blaine's name. She thought it odd how Detective Jorgan seemed so protective of someone who was just another victim of a crime. She sensed it was something that went much deeper, but didn't have a clue as to what that could be and certainly couldn't ask. Maybe what she'd told Blaine about Detective Jorgan possibly having been a victim of some kind of abuse herself wasn't so far from the truth after all.

"After high school, I unfortunately became involved with the wrong crowd. I guess I was considered to be wild… drinking, drugs, you know the story." She let her breath out slowly. "My parents got tired of my attitude and of supporting me. They laid it on the line that I would abide by their rules or be thrown out. I didn't believe them and one day they kicked me out. Just like that. I suppose it was the only thing they could do. I was out of control and tough love was all they had left. At the time I was bitter and angry and vowed I didn't need them."

"Where did you go, Kami?" Jane asked.

"I wasn't worried about finding somewhere to crash. The crowd I ran with—there was always someone who'd give me a place to sleep for the night. Eventually, though, I ended up moving in with a girl named Nancy." She swallowed the lump in her throat. "One night Nancy introduced me to Josh Barnes. I'd never seen him before, but Nancy explained that he was an old friend of hers who'd just moved to the city. She thought Josh and I might hit it off. To use an old and tired cliché, Josh literally swept me off my feet. I fell for him—hard. I honestly don't know how I could've been so naïve, but I suppose it was

117

because all he showed me in the beginning was his soft and gentle side. We were almost inseparable. A few weeks later, I moved in with him." She clenched her hands together tightly.

Casey looked intently at her. "How did you become involved in his business? Were you aware of it before you moved in with him?"

She shook her head as tears filled her eyes. "I thought I was Josh's girl…exclusively. You know—boyfriend, girlfriend thing and that eventually we would marry, settle down, and raise a family." She blinked. "One night, though, things changed when he brought some guys and girls over. I assumed it was just the usual night of partying. We'd do that a few times a week. I didn't know these new friends of his, but that wasn't unusual either. Josh was a friendly guy and he was always meeting new people and bringing them home. He had the kind of charisma that drew people to him." She cast her eyes down. "But that night was different." She drew a shaky breath.

"What happened that night?" Jane asked.

She clenched her hands tightly together. "He asked me to have sex with one of the guys. I was shocked and thought it was a sick joke. It wasn't. He was serious—dead serious." She shuddered at the recollection.

Jane's eyebrows shot up. "He came right out just like that and said he wanted you to take this stranger to bed?"

Kami's face flushed. "Yes," she whispered in an unsteady voice. "At that time, I worshipped Josh. I would've done almost anything for him." Her eyes brimmed with tears. "If this was what it took to make him happy, then I would force myself to do it for him. Because I loved him." She bit her bottom lip. "But I couldn't get over the fact that if he loved me as much as I did him, why would he want me sleeping with other guys. I certainly wouldn't have tolerated his sleeping around and certainly never would have asked him to sleep with one of my friends."

"That was when he became your pimp?" Casey asked.

Her face paled. "I suppose, but it started as something he wanted me to do just one time...at least that's what I thought at the time."

"You had no idea what he expected from you?" Jane asked.

"Not right away." She blew her breath out before continuing. "After that night with his friend he kept telling me that he could make some good money off me."

"How were Josh and you supporting yourselves at that time?" Casey asked.

"Josh didn't like me hanging out anywhere without him. He didn't want me working. I thought he was old-fashioned. As far as I knew, he had a job at some gas station as a mechanic. I didn't know until much later that he was really committing burglaries and then started a small-time drug operation with his friends."

"What happened after you slept with his friend?" Casey asked.

"When he suggested he could make money off me I took it as a joke. But Josh was serious. Every few days he would ask me to sleep with one of his friends. I didn't want to and I told him that. I let him know in no uncertain terms that I only did it that one time, but I did not intend to do it again." She bit her bottom lip. "But Josh can be very persuasive when he wants to be. And like I said, I loved him so much that I would have done almost anything for him. I didn't know his friends were paying him to have sex with me," she choked. "I felt so cheap and degraded when I found out."

119

"How did you find out?" Jane asked.

"I walked in on a conversation with him and one of his so-called friends. I saw the man hand him some money."

"When you realized what Barnes was up to, why didn't you get out then?" Casey asked. "You could have refused to sleep with those men."

She ran a hand through her hair. "I tried. None of my former friends would take me in. I had no money, no job, and nowhere to go. I wish I would have contacted my family, but stupidly I didn't want to give them the satisfaction. Josh continued to take care of me so I kept doing what he wanted. When I finally woke up one day and realized I wanted to make something of my life, it was too late. I knew too much. The sex ring of his was growing bigger and bigger. I never knew how many other girls he'd brought into it either. He's a very intelligent and manipulative man." She looked down at her hands. "He started dressing both of us expensively and even bought a couple of apartment buildings. Including the one I live in. He expanded the business to include politicians and those in power. He has connections everywhere. He billed me as one of his top girls."

"That should certainly make you proud," Casey said with a just trace of sarcasm in her voice.

Kami's eyes misted. "I didn't mean for it to sound that way, because I certainly am not proud. I was just trying to show you the type of organization he runs and the large amounts of money involved. There are many supposed 'pillars of the community' who seek his services and can afford to pay for what he offers. Their reputations would be destroyed if the truth were known. Josh Barnes is definitely not a run-of-the-mill street pimp."

Casey's eyes softened. "I apologize," she said. "I have

no right to pass judgment on you. Did you ever ask Blaine if you could move in with her after you were asked to leave your parents' home? You said you were friends."

"No, Blaine never knew what I was involved in. After high school, I sort of just drifted in and out of her life. I knew she would have helped me as much as she could, but I didn't want her to see what I had resorted to."

She took a deep breath. "Anyway, Josh refused to let me go. Since he was going big time, I had to get off the drugs. After I got clean, I found work as a private secretary, through a connection of Josh's, so it wouldn't look suspicious as to how I could live so well."

"Couldn't you have told someone what was going on since he gave you the freedom to work?" Casey asked.

"No. I was on a tight leash. I was terrified to cross him. I had no idea of who to trust. I was constantly reminded of his connections."

"How did you reconnect with Blaine?" Jane asked.

Kami frowned. "By that time, I'd reconnected with Blaine. I'd run into her somewhere and it was as though I'd never been gone. Josh had allowed me to have dinner or see her for a movie sometimes. So we went on like that for quite a while."

Casey listened intently. "Did you ever invite Blaine to your apartment?"

"Yes, several times."

"Was Barnes there?"

"No. I would only do it when I knew he wouldn't be around."

Jane was thoughtful for a minute. "Did Blaine ever question how you could afford to live in one of the most expensive neighborhoods in Philadelphia?"

"All she knew was that I was a private secretary for a hotshot lawyer."

"And he's one of Barnes' clients," Casey stated.

She nodded.

Casey cocked an eye. "Would you be willing to share his name and every name you know who's involved in this operation?"

Kami cleared her throat. "Yes. I think you'll be surprised at some of them. It only took him two years to go from nothing to what he has now."

"Now, getting back to Blaine," Casey said.

"Recently Josh told me we needed some new blood. He informed me that I would be bringing someone in. I was skeptical because I never knew anything about that part of the organization. He was the only one who brought in new girls. It was important to him to keep the line fresh and his growing client list happy. I'd only been in charge of meeting the girls, after they were medically checked out. If any were on drugs or had any diseases, they were tossed out."

"When you say meeting them, what do you mean?" Jane asked.

"I would show them my apartment and all my designer clothes and impress upon them how they would have the same if they didn't cross the line. But all of those girls came in willingly. They were anxious to please Josh."

"Did any of them ever try to get out?" Casey asked.

Her eyes shifted. "A few."

"What happened to them, Kami?" Jane asked quietly.

Tears rolled down her cheeks. "I never saw them again. I think Josh or one of his connections had them killed. He used them as an example to keep the rest of us in line. No one dared tried to get out after that." She covered her face with her hands and sobbed.

Jane slid a box of tissues across the table. She caught Casey's eye, then waited a few minutes until Kami got herself under control before continuing their questioning.

"So you always wanted to leave but couldn't. Is that correct?" Casey asked.

Kami nodded as she dabbed at her eyes with a tissue. "I had to put on an act. I could never be myself. My life wasn't my own."

"So how did Blaine happen to get involved?" Jane asked.

"Josh knew that Blaine and I were friends. She'd never met him before she moved in. As I said before, Blaine and I would get together for dinner, lunch, the movies, or things like that. Sometimes we'd hang out at her place. Anyway, Josh saw us out one evening. He must have followed me. He became almost obsessed with her. He insisted that I get her to become part of the organization. It didn't matter whether she wanted to or not, it only mattered what *he* wanted." She clutched her coffee cup. "I was going to explain it all to her, but then she was attacked and I never got the opportunity because she was going through enough. I tried to convince Josh to forget about Blaine, but he refused to listen. He'd never forced a girl before and I was terrified for Blaine. I didn't know what to do. I never wanted her to get involved in this." She swallowed hard. "Josh was growing impatient so I had to do something. He has a violent temper and I knew he wouldn't wait much longer, even though I told him she'd just been attacked. I thought if I could stall him for a while maybe I could figure out a way to keep him away from Blaine."

"Is that why when I questioned Blaine you suggested she should stay with you because she was afraid to be alone?"

Casey asked stiffly.

"Yes. Josh had said if I didn't do it then he would take matters into his own hands. The next day Josh met Blaine for the first time when she moved into my apartment." She glanced at Casey.

Jane looked at Casey's stony expression, then back to Kami. "What happened, Kami?"

"When Josh found out that I hadn't told Blaine about the organization, he became extremely irate. He slapped me around and was totally out of control. Blaine tried to run." She swiped at her eyes. "He…he beat and raped Blaine that night." Her voice quivered, then broke. "He's forcing her to entertain almost every night now. He won't let up on her and it's killing her," she sobbed. "Blaine doesn't deserve this." She shivered violently. "I never wanted her mixed up in this." She covered her face with her hands as soft moans wracked her body.

Jane was instantly at her side. She put an arm around the young woman's shoulder. "We'll get him, Kami. I promise you, we'll get the bastard!"

Casey pounded her fist on the table. "How could you do this to her? What kind of a friend are you?"

Kami looked up at her through bleary red swollen eyes. "I'm not proud of myself!" she cried. "I want to help her. That's why I'm here. She keeps fighting Josh, and she'll never get out of this alive!"

"What do you mean?" Casey demanded. "Explain what you mean!"

"He…he has connections. He has people taken care of who betray him. I already told you that."

Jane looked quizzically at Casey. "You said they disappear and you insinuated he's capable of more. Tell us the truth right now, Kami."

"Are you talking about murder…hiring hit men?" Casey demanded.

She nodded. "I'm afraid he'll have someone kill Blaine if he doesn't do it himself," she cried.

"How can you call yourself a friend when you set her up?" Casey shouted. "You didn't have to do it. No matter what you say, you had a choice!"

"Didn't you listen to a word I just said?" Kami asked. "I had no choice. He would have killed me and still ended up with Blaine."

"Calm down, Casey, and give the kid a break, for God's sake! No one forced her to come here and talk to us. She's taking a big risk herself."

Casey stood up, glared at them, and then stalked out of the room. She walked outside into the brisk air filling her lungs until she thought they would burst. She lit a cigarette, slowly blowing the smoke out as her mind went over every word Kami had spoken. She threw her cigarette to the ground and knotted her hands into fists as her anger mounted and seethed inside until she thought she would explode.

****

Blaine slowly opened her eyes. She took a deep breath and held it in before slowly releasing it hoping to alleviate some of the intense pain crushing her ribs. She rested for a few seconds. She had to get help. She glanced around. Where was her cell phone? Earlier she'd had it with her, but it must have fallen during Josh's vicious assault on her. Had he seen it and taken it with him to prevent her from calling for help? Maybe he'd intercepted Kami and she wouldn't be coming back to the apartment. She could lie here all weekend. No one would miss her. Not even her former coworkers. Josh had forced her to quit her job and had moved her things out of her apartment. He knew she wouldn't survive. That's what he'd planned. Kami would return home, find Blaine, and the police would assume someone had broken in and attacked her.

Her body was growing numb with pain. She rolled onto her stomach and inched across the floor. Maybe she could get to the landline phone. After ten minutes, she couldn't go any further and was ready to give up and accept her fate when her eye caught something under the sofa. She mustered up her last bit of strength willing herself not to pass out, and after another twenty minutes made it to the sofa. She reached under the couch and her fingers touched a familiar item. She pulled the phone out. Her head was swimming. She knew it was only a matter of time before she passed out again.

****

Casey walked over to her desk. She glanced at a file folder, picked it up, and then threw it down on the desk. She couldn't bring her emotions under control and she knew she had to and soon. She had to go back into that room and calmly talk to Kami Matthews. Yelling at Kami Matthews and making accusations wasn't helping Blaine. She took a deep breath, and then slowly let it out. Her phone rang, but she ignored it. It persisted ringing until she finally picked it up.

"Detective Jorgan," she barked into the phone.

"Please...please...help...me."

"Who is this?" she asked listening closely to the low, raspy breathing. "I can barely hear you."

"Blaine."

"Blaine? Blaine, what's wrong?" Her voice softened. Fear gripped her heart. Her hand shook.

"Please..."

"Blaine, what's wrong? I can barely hear you." She

waited for an answer, but all she heard was raspy labored breathing. "Blaine, can you hear me?" she called. When she received no response, she slammed the phone down. She ran to the conference room flinging open the door, startling both Kami and Jane.

"Casey, what is it?" Jane asked, grabbing her arm.

Casey's heart pounded in her chest. "It's Blaine. Something's happened to her. We've got to get over there!" Perspiration dotted her brow and her hands were clammy.

Kami jumped to her feet. "My God! What's wrong! What's happened?" she cried.

Casey shook her head back and forth. "I don't know! You stay put. You'll be safe here until we know what's going on." She steered Jane toward the door. "Come on, let's go! We don't have any time to lose!"

****

Casey pounded on the door. "Open the door, Blaine. It's Detective Jorgan!" she called. "Can you hear me, Blaine?" She looked at Jane. "I'm going to break the door in, Blaine. If you can hear me, stand back!"

John was instantly at her side. "That's not necessary." He took a master key from his pocket and inserted it into the lock.

Jane positioned herself by the side of the door with her gun in place as he unlocked the door. "Stay out here," she ordered with a nod in John's direction as she and Casey cautiously entered the apartment. She kept close to the wall as she edged her way into the living room.

Casey was on the opposite wall keeping her eyes focused for any movement. When she reached the living room, she quickly pulled open a closet door. "Blaine, are you here?" she called.

Jane cautiously made her way around the opposite end

of the large room. She stopped when an overturned lamp brushed her foot. She stooped down and saw Blaine's limp arm with her cell phone in her hand. "Casey! Call an ambulance! Hurry!"

Casey ran to her side. "Oh, my God, no!" she cried seeing Blaine's twisted body lying in a heap on the floor. She quickly made the call as she kept her eyes glued on Blaine. Tears stung her eyelids.

"She's got a pulse. Stay with her while I check out the rest of the place," Jane instructed.

"Of course," Casey nodded numbly. "Blaine, can you hear me? It's Officer Jorgan, Blaine."

Blaine's eyelids fluttered but didn't open.

Casey rechecked her pulse. It was weak. "You're going to be all right. An ambulance is on the way." She looked up at Jane who had just walked back into the living room. "It's weak…they'd better hurry."

Jane nodded. "It's all clear...nothing," Jane said. "Whoever did this to her is gone. We'll have to question the doorman. He certainly must know who has been in and out this afternoon." She gently touched Casey's shoulder. "She'll be okay."

Casey shrugged Jane's hand off as she stood up with her back to her. She swiped at the hot heavy tears behind her eyelids. At any moment, she knew that the threatened tears could fall. Masking what she was really feeling was becoming more difficult as each second that ticked by could mean the difference between life and death for her sister. She nervously clenched then unclenched her hands.

"Are you all right?" Jane softly asked. "What is it, Casey? Let me help."

Casey stiffened. "I'm okay," she quickly replied.

Jane sighed. "What's going on with you, Casey? Don't tell me nothing is wrong because I know you well enough to know when something's bothering you. What's the connection with Blaine? It's been obvious from day one on this case that it's been disturbing to you. Come on, it's time to level with me. Let me help, whatever it is."

Casey's shoulders slumped forward. "Just leave me alone. Please? This is my problem and I'll work it out for myself."

"I don't think you can, Casey." A commotion in the hallway interrupted anything else Jane may have wanted to say, much to Casey's relief. "It must be the paramedics." Jane ran to the open door and ushered them in and over to Blaine. They immediately went to work on Blaine.

Casey stood by helplessly watching them as they loaded Blaine onto a stretcher.

****

John glared at the detectives. "How dare you insinuate that I am withholding information. I refuse to answer any more of your ridiculous questions!" He turned away, dismissing them with a shake of his head.

"If you don't want to answer our questions here, maybe you'd prefer to do it at the station." Casey stared coldly at him. "Your choice. Do you want to talk to us here or would you rather come down to the station?"

John smoothed his jacket. "Since my options are limited, I suppose here."

"Give me a list of everyone who visited Kami Matthews' apartment today." Casey tapped her pen against her notepad.

"I could lose my job for releasing this information," he answered.

"And a young woman is lying in the hospital fighting for

her life right now because someone almost beat her to death!" Casey's said.

John took a handkerchief from his breast pocket and mopped the perspiration forming on his brow. "I didn't realize she was so badly injured." Sweat broke out on his chin. "The tenants are quite understandably alarmed at what's happened in Miss Matthews' apartment," he said.

"Who was in Kami Matthews' apartment today?" Jane asked impatiently.

He nervously shifted his eyes.

"Are you employed by Josh Barnes?" Casey demanded.

John cleared his throat. "Yes."

"I'm only going to ask you this once. If you refuse to answer, we'll bring you to the station for questioning. Was Josh Barnes here today?" Jane asked.

"He owns the building so he regularly stops by."

Casey took his arm. "I think you'll be more comfortable answering questions at the station."

John held up a hand. "No, I'll answer. Josh Barnes was the only visitor to the Matthews' apartment today. I know he has a vile temper, but I don't believe that he could do such a contemptible thing as this." His eyes flitted nervously.

Chapter Ten

"What's the next move?" Jane asked Casey as they entered the hospital.

"We have to put that bastard away for good, but first we need to check on Blaine's condition. Hopefully she's out of surgery."

"I hope so too," Jane said seeing the worried expression in Casey's eyes.

They walked over to the nurses' station and after a few minutes of being ignored, Casey tapped loudly on the counter. A heavyset nurse glanced up at her.

"I need some information about a patient," Casey stated. She flashed her badge.

The nurse tucked an escaped strand of graying hair under her cap. "I'm sorry, Detective, we're swamped today. Is this about the accident out on the expressway? They're still bringing victims in."

"No, I need some information about Blaine Kirsten. She was taken into emergency surgery a couple of hours ago," Casey said impatiently.

She checked her computer screen. "She's still in surgery. You can talk to the surgeon when he comes out. It shouldn't be too much longer."

131

Casey was silent as she and Jane seated themselves in the waiting room. She leaned her head back against the chair and closed her eyes.

"Want some coffee?" Jane asked.

"No, thanks." She yawned.

Jane settled back into the seat, picked up a magazine, and then quickly tossed it aside. "You're beat, Casey. Why don't you take a couple of days off and get some rest?"

"How can I? We have to figure out a way to protect Blaine and Kami. We'll need to request someone to guard Blaine's room once she's out of surgery. If what Kami says is true, we have no clue who Josh's connections may be. The only thing we know is the way Kami dresses and the location and furnishings in her apartment means some big bucks are changing hands. This isn't some small-time operation."

Jane noticed the worry lines around Casey's eyes and the deep creases in her forehead. Her eyes, which were usually bright and clear, now had a sadness in them that would cut to the most hardened soul. Jane yearned to help her friend and would do anything to bring back the Casey she knew before they were given the Blaine Kirsten case. She had to try one more time to reach her. "Level with me," she said softly. "We've always been able to confide in each other since the first day we met at the police academy. Please don't hold back on me now, Casey. What's up with this girl? What is it about Blaine that has you so twisted up inside?"

Casey looked at her but kept silent.

Jane gently squeezed Casey's shoulder. "Tell me about it. Talking about it might help, you know?"

Casey drew a deep breath. "I'm so scared for her, Jane." She blinked rapidly.

"I am, too, but in your case it goes deeper, doesn't it?" She searched Casey's eyes, which now were filled with grief.

Casey shifted uncomfortably in her seat. "Once Blaine is well again, everything will be okay. I hate these types of cases, but more than that, I hate men like Josh Barnes. Always one step above the law. He owns these girls, but no one can get him on anything because he lets them come and go."

"Not always at will. He knows their every move, according to Kami and from the little Blaine told us."

"And yet none of the girls dare to turn him in," Casey reminded her.

"Until Kami." Jane eyed her sharply. "Don't play games with me, Casey. I can see right through you."

"Are you a psychic now?" She laughed softly.

"Stop it." Jane said. "This is no joking matter. Your mood swings are really beginning to scare me. Just tell me what you've been keeping bottled up inside. Can't you see how scared I am for you?"

She stiffened. "I can't get into this right now, Jane. You wouldn't understand."

"Try me."

She sighed. "You know how you're always talking about feelings?"

Jane nodded.

"Well, my feelings are very confused right now. Sometimes they completely overwhelm me." She let her breath out in a rush. "I feel like I'm over the edge, hanging on for dear life and I'm losing my grip. I don't know what to do or if I can even do anything." She looked at Jane with glistening eyes.

She patted Casey's hand reassuringly. "I'll help you through this, Casey. Please, just trust me. Whatever it is, you don't have to go through it alone."

She exhaled loudly and ran a hand through her hair.

"There is a vast void in my life that I've always felt. It's almost like the way you feel when you want someone you know you can never have. It becomes an almost all-consuming love, but it isn't real. Poor example, but it's the best I can do right now. My emotions seem to only be real in my dreams. No matter how much I hope, pray, and just plain wish that I could feel fulfilled, I still have to face the harsh, cold reality of life. I wake up every morning and nothing has changed." A tear slid down her cheek. "I'm so empty inside. There's this big hollow hole that will never be filled. I go through the motions every day almost mechanically. I'm so tired."

"You're burning out, Casey. You need some R & R and soon." She reached out to comfort her, but Casey pushed her away.

"You don't really know me, Jane. No one really knows me." She sniffed. "My life is so screwed up. It has been for a very long time."

She watched Casey's expression and knew that Casey had already turned her feelings back off. "Just knowing that someone really does care can make all the difference in the world. You're not alone, Casey. I care. Stan cares." She sat silently and looked up when a surgeon headed their way.

"Hello, Detectives. I understand you're here to discuss Blaine Kirsten?"

"How is she?" Casey asked jumping to her feet. "How did she come through the surgery?"

He shook his head. "She came through the surgery just fine, but we'll be keeping a close eye on her. She has some cracked ribs and a mild concussion. We stopped the internal bleeding and I see no internal damage." He looked at the women. "It appears that she was either struck or kicked with a blunt object." He frowned. "She's been beaten before."

Casey's stomach churned. "Will she be all right?"

He turned to Casey and removed his glasses. "She should be this time. Next time she might not be so lucky. She'll have to stay hospitalized for several days though."

"We need to question her about the attack," Jane said.

He frowned. "She's just come out of surgery. She'll be in recovery for some time. Any questions are going to have to wait until later. Maybe tomorrow."

"Thank you, Doctor," Jane replied. She turned to Casey. "We'd better get back to the station and give Lt. Richardson and Kami the update."

****

Twenty minutes later, they found Kami anxiously pacing back and forth in the conference room where they'd left her hours before. Her neatly pressed suit was now wrinkled and her hair looked like she'd been continuously running her fingers through it.

Her eyes were large and hollow in her ashen face. "How's Blaine?" She grabbed Casey's hand. "Please tell me," she said in a frightened voice. "Is she okay?"

"Blaine was severely beaten." Casey's voice was almost inaudible in the quiet room.

Kami's hand flew to her mouth. "Oh, my God!"

"She'll be all right." She sat down and rubbed her burning eyes. "Do you still want to help us?"

"Of course," she answered. "Did Blaine say that Josh was responsible for this?"

"Blaine didn't say anything. She's still in recovery. But I know he did this to her."

"Can't you just arrest him?" Kami asked searching her eyes.

She shook her head. "You should know better than that,

Kami. We need to get Barnes on more than a brutal assault. He'd be back on the streets in no time. Besides, Blaine would have to identify him as her assailant and at the moment, she's not able to do it. Even if she was, she may be too terrified to do it." She tapped her fingertips on the edge of the table. "What do you think the odds are of her testifying against him now?"

Kami frowned. "You're right. Blaine would never do it. She'd be too frightened now. He'd kill her and me." She looked at Casey. "I don't think she would ever cooperate with you anyway, Detective Jorgan. Maybe she would with Detective Adams, though."

"Why not with me?" Casey asked in surprise. "I'm the one she called for help."

"I don't know." Kami twisted her necklace and shrugged. "I don't want to hurt your feelings, but she doesn't feel comfortable around you."

Jane saw the hurt in Casey's eyes. She leaned her elbows on the table as she waited for Kami to continue.

"Because?" Casey asked.

"Blaine isn't convinced that you care about what happens to us because of what Josh has forced us to do...especially me."

"What I personally think or do not think about either of you has nothing whatsoever to do with the matter at hand. Right now we've got a case to solve and you are the only one who can help us." She placed her hands gently on Kami's shoulders. "We need to put Barnes away for good. We've got to! It's going to be a big risk on your part, Kami. I won't kid you, but right now you're the only one who can do it." Her eyes narrowed. "And just for the record, I'm not judging you or Blaine. You were both forced even though he used different tactics on the both of you. But the result is the same. I care

136

about your well-being and Blaine's."

Kami swallowed the lump in her throat. "I'll do whatever you say. I only want to help Blaine. That's my top priority. That's why I came here in the first place today."

Casey stared intently at the young woman. "Kami," she said in a low voice. "I'm sorry for coming down so hard on you before. When this is over, you'll understand my position. That's all I can say for now."

She nodded.

"We'll protect you, Kami. Detective Jorgan and I need to formulate a plan," Jane stated. "We've already got someone at the hospital posted outside of Blaine's room."

"I don't think Josh would dare to do anything now with Blaine in the hospital. That would be stupid," Kami said.

"You said yourself that he has connections, which we need you to make a list of." Casey slid a notepad and pen across the table to Kami. "He's not going to give her a chance to talk."

Jane looked at Casey while Kami worked on the list of names. "Casey, if Lt. Richardson agrees, I think it would be best if you stayed with Kami."

"Are you agreeable to it, Kami," Casey asked.

"Yes."

Casey flashed a slight smile. "If Lt. Richardson okays it, then I'll do it," she answered.

"Good. I'll also let Lt. Richardson know that you're making a list, Kami." Jane patted Kami's shoulder. "We'll get through this."

After Jane left, Casey turned to Kami. "How much do you know about Blaine's background? What was her upbringing like?"

Kami stopped writing and looked at Casey. "She told

me she was adopted when she was only six months old. Her adoptive parents were great and she had a pretty decent childhood. They weren't rich, but she had nice clothes and all the things that were important. In school, she was a little shy, but everyone who knew her liked her."

"Did the Kirstens have any other children, biological or adopted?"

"No, just Blaine. No other relatives either that she ever mentioned. They doted on her."

"Since Blaine was adopted, did she ever mention any biological brothers or sisters?"

"She never mentioned any, but then she was only a baby when she was adopted. If she has any, she's not aware of it." She was thoughtful for a moment. "Blaine used to have this dream every night about someone looking for her. It never made much sense. All she knows about her past is that her parents had been killed in a car accident. Nothing was ever mentioned about any siblings. She was bothered by nightmares for years." She frowned. "I don't know what made me think of that now." She toyed with the pen in her hand. "It would be nice if she had someone with all she's been through."

"Did she know her name before she was adopted?"

"No," Kami replied. "If she did, I know she would have told me because it would have helped her."

"What do you mean?"

"It wasn't until her adopted parents died that Blaine began to wonder about her biological family, if there were any. She tried to run some Internet searches but couldn't find anything." She sighed. "It's difficult when you don't even have a name to work with." She looked at Casey. "Is there any way you could find out if she has any family? I mean you have resources here to do some searches. There's got to be a biological cousin or someone even remotely related to her out there somewhere. She's been alone for so long. She needs to know that she has roots somewhere. It would mean so much to her. Even if she finds out that she has no living relatives left, I know it would mean a lot to her to at least be able to connect somewhere. Not to take anything away from the Kirstens, but a person should still know where she comes from."

"I'll try, but I can't promise anything when there's not much to go on."

"Anything you can do will be helpful. Blaine has had a hard life. I mean, with her real parents dying, then her adoptive parents dying, and her being attacked. But the worst is what Josh has done to her."

"Yes," Casey agreed. "No one deserves all she's been through."

Kami was reflective for a moment. "Did you know that Blaine is a beautiful artist? She wants to know where she got her artistic ability, but mostly where she got her yen for Italian food." She laughed. "But seriously, she does wonderful sketches and paintings."

Casey smiled. "You really are concerned for her well-being."

"Yes, I am." She's the best friend I've ever had."

Casey patted Kami's hand. "I promise as soon as we take care of Barnes I'll work on finding Blaine's roots."

Jane beamed as she entered the room. "Good news! It's all set!"

Casey gave Kami the thumbs-up.

Chapter Eleven

Casey laid her suitcase on the bed and rummaged through it, finally pulling out a pair of jeans and a sweater. She removed her dress, slipped her casual outfit on, and then put on a pair of tennis shoes. She brushed her hair back, then set her hairbrush on the dresser and walked into the living room, where Kami had set a plate of sandwiches on the coffee table.

"What time did you say Barnes is coming over?" she asked.

"Eight o'clock." She drew a nervous breath. "I'm scared, Detective Jorgan. I'm afraid he'll suspect something."

Casey smiled reassuringly. "Don't be. I won't let anything happen to you. Remember, pretend I'm not even here. I'm just going to observe his operation for a few days. We want to get as many on his list as we can." She picked up a sandwich and took a bite. "This is good."

"Thanks." Kami took a few nibbles from a sandwich then set it back on the plate.

After they finished eating, Casey rechecked the wiretaps while Kami cleaned up the dishes.

Casey closely observed Kami as she moved through the rooms of the large apartment. She was beginning to thaw where Kami was concerned knowing what a risk Kami was taking to protect Blaine. Kami's intentions were sincere and genuine. She was putting her own life at risk to protect her friend.

"I'd better get into position," she said a few minutes before eight o'clock. "Remember that every sound in every room is being recorded. Barnes won't even be aware of it, but I'll be able to hear everything." She patted Kami's back. "It'll be okay. I promise."

Ten minutes later, the familiar knock sounded on the door. Kami stood straight, took a deep breath, then slowly walked over and opened it.

Josh pushed his way past her and sauntered into the living room. He took his time mixing a drink. "You're going to make some big bucks tonight, baby." He smiled. "Bernard Miller is going to pay double for just a little extra time with you." He took a gulp of his drink. "Of course…" He grinned, turning to face her. "There is one little catch."

"What?" she asked uneasily.

He snorted. "Old Bernard must have been watching some hard core porn because he's got some kinky stuff planned."

"I won't do S&M," Kami said determinedly.

"I hope I'm not hearing you right, baby," he said gruffly. "You'll do as I say and give the client what he wants. He's paying big bucks to have his fantasies fulfilled by you tonight."

"You always prided yourself on running a clean operation," she insisted.

"Sexual desires change and you need to go along with it, Kami." He studied her. "Don't push me tonight. I'm not in the mood." His voice grew cold. "Blaine had to be taught a lesson, but I hear she's recuperating nicely. For now." He smiled. "You were scheduled to have the night off, but you have to fill in for Blaine, so you may be working double time for a while. Miller wanted to try Blaine, but he said he'd settle for you...the familiar." He winked at her. "Blaine's going to be a good little money-maker. It's unfortunate, though, that she isn't bright enough to remember who the boss is." He grabbed Kami's wrist. "I certainly wouldn't want anything to happen to you, if you get my meaning." He released her. "I don't want you to talk to those detectives anymore either. Do I make myself clear?"

"Blaine is my roommate, so they had to question me."

"What did you tell them?"

"Nothing. How could I know what happened to Blaine? I wasn't here, I was out shopping."

"I warned John, too, but he assured me that he didn't tell them anything. He only let them into the apartment."

"Does it ever bother you, Josh, knowing that you and I once were a couple?" She lowered her eyes. "I used to be madly in love with you back then. What happened to you?"

"Nothing happened to me, baby. I was never in love with you. Plain and simple. But I knew if I kept you around long enough, you might become useful to me. And you have." He set his glass down. "Face it, Kami. These guys certainly couldn't attract young beauties like my girls on their own. In addition, they can't afford the risks of street prostitutes. Besides, they want something higher-classed. I give them first-class whores. The best money can buy."

"Didn't you ever care about any woman?"

He sneered. "The only thing women have going for them is how they can perform in the sack. It's what's between their legs and the size of the chest that matters to me."

Kami felt queasy. "Josh, what if Blaine turns you in? What's going to happen to us?"

He laughed. "I sincerely doubt she's that stupid, but

even if she did, I'd get off," he answered confidently. "Then our beautiful little Blaine would be laid to rest permanently." He roughly pulled her to him. "You're not thinking of doing something stupid, are you, baby?" His eyes bore through her.

"No. No, of course not, Josh." She smiled weakly. "Never."

"Oh, I just remembered something." He chuckled. "A couple of prospective clients are interested in my services, but they want something a little different. Something I've never offered before."

"What?" Kami asked.

"They want two girls." He winked. "They won't be participating, though."

Kami's eyes grew wide. "What are you saying?"

He grinned at her. "When Blaine gets on her feet again, I think you and she will become even better friends. If you know what I mean."

"I'm not sure," she answered slowly not wanting to believe what he was saying.

"Since as far as I know, you haven't, and I presume Blaine hasn't, ever made love to a woman, you and she can get together to see what it's like." He was silent for a moment. "In front of me."

Kami furiously shook her head. "Never! That is where I draw the line, Josh!"

He laughed. "You just might enjoy it."

"I won't sleep with another woman."

"It's not just any woman, it's your best friend."

"Which makes it even worse," she hissed. "It would be different if Blaine and I were lesbians, but we're not," she emphatically stated. "Blaine won't do it either. Find some girls who are lesbians, but not me or Blaine."

He tilted his head as he looked down on her. "You can

and you will do whatever I say." He mixed another drink. "There's one more thing I want to talk to you about."

She drew her lips tightly together. "I'm afraid to ask what it is."

"Nothing for you to worry about. When Blaine is discharged from the hospital, I want you to take her for a Brazilian wax. Also, I'll arrange to have her tested for the usual."

"I don't think she'll be getting out for a while. And when she does she'll have a long recuperation."

"Not too long." His eyes narrowed. "I just had a thought. If those detectives try to question you again, refuse."

"I can't refuse."

"You can and you will. If they persist, I have someone who can make life very difficult for them. I don't like them poking their noses where they don't belong. Especially that redhead." He grunted. "I must say, though, that I wouldn't mind getting her in the sack." He licked his lips. "She's quite a looker."

Kami wanted to tell him to go to hell, but knew she had to play along with him to prevent him from becoming suspicious. She rolled her eyes. "Josh, you're terrible!" She forced herself to smile. "You can always count on me," she lied.

"That's my girl." His voice grew soft. "Make sure to treat Bernard Miller extra special tonight. There'll be a nice bonus in it for you." He ran his fingers up and down her arm.

Kami's flesh crawled with his touch. He wasn't human, ice ran through his veins. She smiled at him again. "Of course, I will."

"That's my girl. I wish I could watch this performance. It makes me hot just thinking about it." He rubbed his crotch as he glanced at his wristwatch.

****

Casey boiled as she listened to the conversation. Barnes' presumed self-importance made her want to puke. What a narcissist. She couldn't wait until that bastard was in prison. She was shocked when she heard the name Bernard Miller. He was currently running for a seat in the senate. His television ads showed him smiling as he stood looking at his wife and adult children. According to the ad, he was a devoted husband and father and would stand up to corruption. She wondered how his family would feel when the truth came out about him. She knew Josh's clients would only get a slap on the wrist. But the publicity would be enough to end their careers and probably their marriages too. Justice would be served in the end.

She thought about the consequences if she quietly made her way into the living room, snuck up behind him, and put a bullet into his head before he knew what hit him. This line of thinking was treading dangerous territory and she knew she had to force herself to use all the self-control she could muster to stay put. One wrong move and she would blow the case putting not only her own life at risk, but Kami's as well.

Her ears perked up when she heard another man's voice join the conversation. *Must be Miller*, she thought. It would be difficult listening to the bedroom scene, but she knew it would be more difficult for Kami having to perform sexual acts with the knowledge that countless others would be hearing the tape later.

****

Kami led Miller to her bedroom. "What do you want?" she asked after she closed the door. "Josh said you had something different in mind for tonight." She forced herself to sound seductive.

145

His pudgy hands hungrily tore her clothes from her, exposing her naked body. His hands traveled up and down her bare flesh roughly squeezing her breasts. Kami's face flushed a deep pink as he whispered obscenities in her ear, and then slid his tongue up and down her neck. She squeezed her eyes shut trying not to look at him, but his image stayed in her mind and she still clearly saw his round face and small penetrating beady eyes. How would she ever survive this night with him, she wondered.

****

Josh fixed himself another drink as he waited for Kami and Miller to exit the bedroom. His breath quickened as he imagined what Miller was doing with Kami. He envisioned Kami lying on her silk sheets, her head slightly propped up on a pillow. Her breasts slowly moving up and down with every breath she took. His mind forced his eyes to travel down her silky body to the luscious treasure between her legs. He loved the feel and taste of Kami. He always had. If there was any woman who could have made him want to settle down, it was Kami. But he'd never tell her that. It didn't matter anyway. His lust for money overruled his heart, and he soon realized that Kami was better used as a source of income instead of a lover. He'd recognized early on in their relationship that she'd do anything for him—so many times she'd told him that her life would be empty without him in it. She was easy to mold and manipulate into the sexually responsive woman he desired her to be. He smiled wryly. He had to admit, though, he'd never found another woman with her sexual passion and drive—one that almost matched his own.

His wandering eye wouldn't allow him to be faithful to just one woman though. If someone sparked his attention, he knew he had to bed her, and he always got his way one way or

146

the other. His money and power bought him any woman he wanted even against her protests. He complacently thought about all the beauties that had passed in and out of his bed. Sometimes he kept some of them around for a while for his own personal pleasure before passing them on to his ever-increasing client list.

Two hours later Kami walked into the living room with a beaming and very satisfied-looking Miller who had an arm wrapped casually around her waist as they made their way over to Josh.

"She's some kind of woman," Miller said, perspiration marking his thick eyebrows. He smacked his lips together. "Whew! She brought all of my wildest fantasies to life."

Josh smiled at her. "I take it you're pleased then."

"I'll have to do a repeat of tonight more often," Miller answered as he squeezed Kami's shoulder.

Kami stiffened at his touch. His pudgy fingers on her bare flesh sickened her almost as much as his looks did. His small eyes looked hungrily at her as the sweat from his bushy brows descended down toward his large nose. His two large nostrils made him look like a pig. She covered her mouth for a moment with her hands as dry heaves tried to make their way up her throat. "How much was this worth?" she asked coldly a few minutes later. "I was asked to do some things that are way out of the norm." Her eyes lowered concealing her shame.

"Fifteen hundred," Josh answered as he took the money from Miller.

"And worth every cent," Miller added obviously thinking his compliment would make her feel better, Kami thought, as he turned his head and grinned at her. But it didn't. She felt dirty and cheap. She'd just performed some of the most perverted acts one human being could perform on another.

"Fifteen hundred dollars!" Kami exclaimed. Her face reddened. "I can't do what I did tonight ever again," she whispered. "It's too humiliating."

Josh's hand clamped tightly on her wrist as he turned to Miller. "Don't mind her, I think it's a PMS thing," he stated firmly.

"No, it's not! No one should have to do what he asked me to do," she said defiantly.

Josh's jaw twitched. "I'm sorry, Bernard, I must apologize for her rude behavior."

"No problem." He turned to Kami. "You've taken twenty years off my life tonight. We *will* repeat this next week."

"She'll be ready." He walked Bernard Miller out.

Kami slumped onto the sofa, so engrossed in her thoughts that she didn't hear Josh come back into the room until he spoke.

"I told you that you command a high price." He smiled. "Don't worry, I have a bonus for you." He peeled off a few bills from the roll he held in his hand and handed them to her.

She held the money in her hand as a tear slowly trickled from her eye and made its way down her cheek

Josh rolled his eyes. "Why are you crying? It's not as though you've just lost your virginity." He touched her cheek then roughly turned her head until she was facing him. "I should be angry with your rudeness to Bernard Miller, but I'll let you off the hook this time. However, if you ever talk to him or any other client the way you did tonight, you'll be sorry!" He let her go. "Well, baby, I've got to check on my other girls."

She shuddered as she nodded her head. She was surprised

148

that Josh had let her off the hook so easily, but knew that somewhere down the road, his memory would recall this exchange and without warning she would be punished.

"I'll see you in a couple of days."

She lifted an eyebrow. "I won't be working, then?"

He put his overcoat on. "I've got to go out of town on business." He chucked her under the chin. "You be a good girl and rest up. I've got several exciting nights lined up for you when I get back." He softly kissed her lips. "Also, don't forget what I mentioned earlier about you and Blaine working together."

****

Casey waited until she heard the apartment door close, then cautiously made her way into the living room. Before she even saw Kami's face she knew the shame and humiliation the young woman felt. Her heart opened up to her.

"Is it still recording?" Kami asked.

"No, I turned it off." Casey sat next to her. "Can I fix you a drink?"

Kami shook her head as hot tears trickled down her cheeks.

Casey shifted uneasily wondering how to comfort her. "It's going to be all right, Kami," she said softly.

She gulped. "I feel so cheap and dirty," she sobbed. "You heard it all. This is what we go through night after night!" She buried her face in her hands. "But tonight was worse. He's getting sicker. God only knows what he'll have in mind next."

"Yes, I did hear everything, Kami, but I understand why you have to do it. I also heard Josh Barnes. You're right. He doesn't give you a choice." She patted Kami's shoulder then handed her a tissue. "I wonder how he'd feel if he knew I was listening and how he'll feel when he goes to trial and these tapes are heard by judge and jury."

"Don't we have enough on him right now?"

Casey's brow furrowed. "We don't know how big his organization is, Kami. The list you gave us is a big help, but if we take him now, he probably won't even serve time. We want to topple his whole organization."

Kami twisted the damp bills she still held in her hand. "I'll never get out of this racket!" She flashed the money in front of Casey's eyes. "Pretty good, huh? Look at this place!" She stood up frantically waving her arms around. "I actually have coworkers envying my address and wishing they could trade places with me," she bitterly spat out. "If they knew what my life was really like, they wouldn't be so envious. I have everything, but I don't want any of it anymore. I wish I could go back to the way things were before this—before Josh. I want my self-respect back. I can't stand the person I've become." She ran her hand through her hair. "I can't take this anymore! I hate myself!" she shrieked. She crumbled in a heap on the sofa, her shoulders heaving up and down as sobs wracked her body.

Casey protectively put her arms around her. "Kami, how long have you been in this business?" she quietly asked.

"Almost five years," she replied through sobs.

Casey's eyebrows shot up. "My God!" she exclaimed. "Well, at least you know it'll soon be over. I promise you that."

She bit her trembling lips. "Can I ask you something, Detective Jorgan?"

"Of course."

She dabbed at her eyes. "I know that you don't like me very much and I don't blame you. What is it about me that you don't like?"

"That's not true, Kami. I admit I was quick to judge you,

and I apologize for my misconceived conceptions about you. What you are doing for us takes a lot of courage and strength. And courage and strength are the two things I admire most in another. After honesty."

"I'll do whatever it takes to free Blaine from this filthy life. I don't blame you for your initial impression of me. I acted so pompous and rude, but I had to. I was scared. I thought Blaine was going to tell you what was going on and I couldn't let her do that. I'm not really the person I pretended to be." She swallowed hard.

Casey patted her shoulder. "I think we're even. I was pretty rough on you too, and I wasn't willing to give you a chance. In fact, I thought you might try to pull a fast one on me tonight with Barnes," she admitted. "I'm sorry for doubting you, Kami."

"I wouldn't do that," Kami said in a hurt tone of voice.

"I know you wouldn't. That's the point I'm trying to make." She smiled. "We've both got to learn to trust each other. That's the only way we'll bring Josh down."

Kami flashed a weak smile. "I know." She shifted her eyes. "It's not easy doing what Josh forces me to do."

"I know that, Kami."

"I used to think about suicide," she stated bluntly. "Sometimes late at night I would lie in my bed and think how easy it would be to just end it all. I thought death would be the only way I would ever be rid of Josh Barnes."

Casey shuddered. "I'm glad you didn't attempt that, Kami, even though I can understand why you would have felt it was your only option." Her voice grew stronger. "This will all be behind you soon and you'll be able to live the life you should be leading."

"I hope so." Her eyes teared up again. "It's disgusting

what he said he wants Blaine and me to do together. I'd kill myself first before I would ever put her through that."

"It won't get that far. I promise. Do you know all of the clients he does business with?"

She frowned. "Not all of them. He's always bringing in new business. That's why none of us can just leave when we feel like it."

"Let me fix you something to eat," Casey offered.

"I'm not very hungry, but thanks anyway."

"I make the best scrambled eggs in the state of Pennsylvania," Casey tempted.

Kami smiled. "Then how can I refuse?"

****

"Did you get a clean tape?" Jane asked looking up from her paperwork as Casey hurried to her desk the following morning.

"I sure did. Barnes is going out of town for a couple of days. Lt. Richardson has agreed to keep an undercover with Kami. You should have seen the look on his face when he heard the tape." She swallowed hard. "Jane, you would never in a million years believe what that bastard subjects those girls to. And to think that some of our most endeared citizens of the community are the ones who are keeping him in business." She threw some notepads in her desk drawer. "We've got to get over to the hospital to check on Blaine. Are you ready to go or do you need a few more minutes to finish up?"

"Wait a minute. I want to know how you and Kami got along and why you're not with her right now." She stared at Casey. "Has something happened that I don't know about?"

"I'm taking a day or two off," she replied. "As for Kami, well, what can I say? I was wrong about her. She's a good kid trying to get out of a bad situation—alive." She stuffed a

152

couple of memos into her jeans' pocket, and then smoothed her jacket. "Come on, let's go."

"What's the hurry?"

"Jane, if you heard what I did last night it would make your skin crawl! Barnes is one sick bastard. We've got to get that son of a bitch and put him away for good." Her face was red with anger. "Blaine can't go through any more of this!"

Jane eyed her sharply. "It always comes back to Blaine, doesn't it? I'm concerned about her too, but I'm just as concerned for Kami and all the other girls in his operation. "She stood up." I don't know what your problem is, Casey, but I suggest that you talk to someone. You've got a very strange obsession with that young woman. What are you going to do next? Stalk her? What is it about Blaine Kirsten that has you in so much turmoil?"

"Leave it alone, Jane! I'm sick and tired of your self-righteous attitude! What kind of a cop are you? Ever since we've begun this case you've had a gun pointed to my head just waiting to pull the trigger!"

Jane flushed. "Keep your voice down. There's no need to shout!" she hissed.

"Hey, Detectives, who's going to throw the first punch?" someone called out. A ripple of laughter came from the other detectives as all eyes centered on Jane and Casey.

"Don't you have anything better to do? This is between my partner and me!" Casey called back.

"Sounds like it," a detective said nudging his partner.

"Mind your own business!" Casey steamed, and then turned with hands on hips to face Jane. "Okay, let's get this all out in the open!" She pointed a finger at her. "I'll tell you what you think you have to know just to get you off my fucking back, but as soon as this case is wrapped up, we're through! I won't work with you ever again!" Her body trembled as she sank into her chair.

"Fine," Jane answered in a lower tone of voice. She assumed that Casey was only making idle threats. She certainly wouldn't let their friendship go down the drain over a case. She hoped that when Casey's head was clearer she would see that Jane only wanted to share whatever pain she was carrying, not to cause her further pain. She had to play along with her for now though.

"After we wrap up this case, I'll personally talk to Lt. Richardson and explain to him that we can no longer work as a team," she said in what she perceived to be a convincing tone of voice.

Casey eyed her suspiciously. "You think I'm kidding, that as soon as all of this blows over we'll go back to being buddy-buddy. Well, you're wrong this time. I've got too much riding on this, and quite frankly I'm fed up with your constant criticisms and nosiness into my private affairs."

Her words stung, but Jane knew deep down that Casey didn't mean it. "So tell me." She sat on the edge of her desk and folded her hands across her chest.

Casey cleared her throat. "You really have to know, don't you?"

Jane nodded as she watched the nervous twitch in Casey's jaw.

Casey rubbed her eyes, and then stared evenly at her. "Blaine Kirsten is my sister."

Jane's jaw dropped. "What?" She was shocked. "Now I know you've lost it! Casey, I know you've been looking for your sister, but why in God's name do you think Blaine Kirsten is that person?"

Casey put her head in her hands. "I knew you'd say that.

You know I've been looking for my baby sister for years. Well, I found her. But instead of sharing my joy and pain, you refuse to believe me." Tears brimmed in her eyes as she rose. "I've got to get to the hospital. Are you coming or not?"

Jane slowly exhaled. "We've got to discuss this, Casey."

"What's to discuss?"

She grabbed Casey's arm. "You can't just lay something like this on me without an explanation!" she whispered. "How do you know for certain that Blaine Kirsten is your sister?"

She blinked. "I have the proof. I've had it for some time now," she answered in a calmer voice.

"Why didn't you say anything?" Jane demanded.

"I wanted to…I wanted to meet her and then tell the world," she said in a quiet voice. "Before I could, though, we were handed her case."

"You're absolutely sure that she is your sister?"

"Forget it!" She shook her head. "I'm sorry I told you as much as I did." Her voice once again grew cold.

"I'm coming over to your apartment tonight whether you like it or not," Jane said. "We need to discuss this."

"Sorry, I have a date."

Jane grabbed her wrist. "I'm also going to ask the lieutenant to pull you off the case. You're too emotionally involved, especially if what you've just told me about Blaine Kirsten is true, you shouldn't even be involved in her case."

"You're going to do *what*?" Casey cried. "You would sink that low?" Tears streamed down her face. "We're done! This is it!" she raged, not caring that everyone's eyes were on her. "This is my case!" she shouted as she stormed out of the station.

****

Casey drove slowly around the city, trying to figure

155

out what to do next. She couldn't believe that Jane had turned on her. In the past, they had put their lives on the line for one another and had been like sisters, but now it was over. She pounded her fist on the steering wheel. Why did things always have to be so hard for her? "Dammit!" she muttered. "For once I would love a little peace in my life," she moaned.

She thought back to the day her parents had died. She was seven then. She could still clearly see in her mind the semi directly in front of them. It seemed like they'd been driving for hours and she'd grown tired and irritable. Her mother kept reassuring her that they would be arriving soon, but Casey couldn't recall where their destination was. She did remember her mother's beautiful auburn hair lifted gently by the breeze coming through the open window and the faint scent of her perfume. Her father was tall with the bluest eyes she'd ever seen and his brown wavy hair had specks of auburn in it. Everyone always marveled at Casey's likeness to her father, and how the baby resembled her mother. She'd been proud to be a replica of her father even though her mother was beautiful with delicate features and baby-soft skin.

Casey loved the car trips with her parents, and especially loved being a big sister. She sat in the backseat reading a picture book. Her baby sister Blaine was in a car seat next to her. Her parents always sang along to the songs on the radio and she could still hear their voices and those songs echoing in her memories.

She blinked. Her mind took her back. She'd never forget her mother's piercing screams as the semi in front of them suddenly braked. Casey's mind was suspended as though in slow motion and no sounds would come from her throat. She was scared…she wanted to crawl to the front seat and onto her mother's lap and bury her face in her mother's comforting chest. She sat frozen as she watched the back of the truck coming closer and closer. In one split second, in a blazing fury of squealing tires, twisted metal, and broken glass, her happy, carefree childhood came to a halt. She didn't remember anything after they crashed into the back of the semi. All she remembered was waking up in the hospital. Miraculously she and her infant sister had escaped with only a few scratches and bruises, but her parents had died instantly.

After a thorough investigation, it was discovered that there were no living relatives, so she had been sent to a home for girls. Blaine had been adopted almost immediately. Every day Casey pleaded and cried to see her sister, but no one would listen to her. She decided then and there that she wouldn't rest until she found her only living blood relative. When she was thirteen, she knew that she wanted to go into police work. She wanted to be the best cop in the country, and no one could take her mind from that goal. She worked long, grueling hours, the promotions soon followed, and when she made detective, it had been a dream come true. She loved her work and couldn't imagine doing anything else that would fill her with such a sense of pride and accomplishment.

She had planned to take her vacation next month, contact Blaine, and share the news with her. Then Lt. Richardson had given Jane and her the Kirsten case throwing a wrinkle in her plans. When she met Blaine for the first time, though, there was no doubt that she was the baby sister who'd been taken from her. Staring at Blaine was like being swept back in time looking through her seven-year-old eyes at her mother.

She pulled into the hospital parking lot. Once inside the hospital, she briskly walked to Blaine's room.

"How's it going, kid?" she asked as she quietly entered the room. As she neared Blaine's bed, she wasn't prepared for the sight that greeted her.

Blaine smiled faintly. "The doctor says I'm doing better than I look." She raised her eyebrows. "You figure it out."

Casey laughed. "You sure had me worried the other day." She pulled a chair to the side of the bed. "I need to talk to you about something, Blaine," she said gently.

Blaine let out a tired sigh. "If it's about Josh, I can't, Detective Jorgan. I'm sorry."

Casey frowned. "Look, kid, if you don't want my help, then why do you call me every time you're in trouble?" She studied Blaine's face for a reaction.

Her eyes shifted. "I don't know. I do want your help, but I'm scared." She coughed and then winced in pain. "Oh, that hurts. Is Kami all right?"

Casey's heart felt like it would break in two. Blaine looked so pale and vulnerable lying against the stark white sheets. The visible parts of her body were discolored and swollen. "I want to talk to you about her."

"She's all right, isn't she?" she asked fearfully.

She nodded. "Yes, she's fine. She's working with us, Blaine. She's going to help us get Barnes."

"I didn't think she'd really go through with it."

"Well, she did. And do you know why?" She stared into Blaine's eyes. "For you. She cares that much. She put her life on the line for you because she feels responsible for what's happened to you."

"Will she be safe?"

"She's under police protection and I'm staying with her. We've got the whole place wired. Do you want out, Blaine? Now's your chance."

"Of course I do, but what do you want me to do?"

"You have to help us put him away. He almost killed

you and now is your chance to stand up and fight back. I want him behind bars for the rest of his natural life."

"Okay," she finally whispered.

"Okay, what?"

"I'll do whatever it takes."

Casey jumped to her feet. "Good. I knew you wouldn't let us down. Everything will be okay, Blaine. I promise you." She squeezed her hand and then quickly dropped it.

Blaine cleared her throat and looked uneasily at Casey. "Can I ask you a question?"

"Anything."

"It's personal."

"Ask away."

She frowned. "You act so much like me sometimes. I get embarrassed when I share my true feelings with someone. You know what I mean? Like when you want to compliment someone, but you feel real stupid because you don't know how to say it. Then if you do say something, it comes out sounding phony and you wished you'd have just kept your mouth shut in the first place?"

Casey smiled. "Yeah, that fits me perfectly." She sat back down. "So is that what you wanted to ask me?"

"No." Her face reddened. "Did you hear…you said the place is wired—" her voice trailed off in an embarrassed silence.

Casey's jaw twitched. "Blaine, I was hiding in the apartment. Yes, I heard Kami and her client."

Blaine's eyes filled with tears. "Then you know how awful it is."

"Yes, I do," she said softly. "Blaine, Kami told me something personal about you."

"What?"

"That you are adopted and have been searching for any possible family."

Blaine burst into tears. Casey moved to the edge of the bed. She wished she could tell her now that she no longer was alone.

"I just want to connect somewhere, have someone who really cares." She sniffed. "Everything is so messed up. I sometimes think I'm a jinx or something. Both sets of my parents are dead and I feel so alone."

Casey put her arm around the young woman and held her as she cried. After several minutes, Blaine took the tissues Casey offered and wiped her eyes. "I'm sorry. I don't usually break down like this. Thank you for understanding, Detective Jorgan."

Casey stood up. "Anytime you feel like talking, Blaine, I'm a good listener." She squeezed Blaine's hand. "I'd better go now and let you get some rest. I'll keep you posted. Don't worry about anything, okay? Concentrate on getting well. You and Kami are well protected."

****

"Honey, what's bothering you?" Stan asked.

Jane listlessly stirred her coffee. "It's Casey. I don't know how to help her, Stan. I forced her to tell me something she didn't want to, and now she's barely speaking to me. I can live with that, but I can't live with how this case we're working on is eating her alive. It's a personal conflict for her. I told her that I was going to have Richardson pull her off the case." She sipped her coffee. "I don't know what to do. I'm only trying to help, but the more I say the worse I'm making matters and pushing her further away."

Stan looked sympathetically at her. "Keep the lines of communication open with her, honey. You two have been

160

friends for far too long to let anything come between you."

"That's what I'm trying to do, but she's shutting me out." She tugged at her chin. "I'm scared for her."

"Just be there for her. That's all you can do." He got to his feet. "Would you like me to talk to her?"

She smiled as she grabbed his hand and brought it to her lips. "No, but thanks for offering. If you talked to her, she would really think she couldn't trust me anymore. I've got to keep her secret…for now, anyway."

"Well, let's go to bed. You'll feel better in the morning."

"I'll be there in a minute."

"I might be sleeping by then." He winked.

Chapter Twelve

Casey stood in front of her living room window, watching lightning streak across the sky. She hoped Greg would arrive before it started storming. She hadn't seen him for weeks and she missed him. They were good compatible friends and made no romantic overtures to one another. Nevertheless, they had a strong sexual attraction for each other. Casey was more relaxed in a noncommitted relationship. After the breakup of her marriage, she had vowed to never again allow herself to get tangled in another emotional relationship.

The lightning flashed brighter. She saw Greg's gray Lexus pull up in front of her apartment building just as the rain began to pelt against the window. She watched as he got out of the car and dashed into the lobby. Minutes later, she met him at the door with a glass of wine.

"You're looking as beautiful as ever, Casey," he said as he appreciatively took in her body, clad in a silk gown which Casey knew revealed every curve.

"Thank you, Greg. I'm sorry I called you on such short notice," she said as they sat next to one another on her sofa.

"No problem. Lawyers need a night off too," he said with a laugh.

"Yes they do." She settled back into the sofa. "The past

few days have been hell, Greg. I feel like I'm in a pressure cooker." She smiled contentedly as he ran his hand up and down her arm. "Tonight I need to unwind."

"I'm at your service," he said as he slipped his sports coat off. "What's gotten you so tensed up?" he asked as he nibbled on her earlobe.

"That's nice," she sighed, snuggling closer to him. "A case I'm working on is really tearing me apart. But I don't want to talk about that right now." She smiled seductively as she traced his finely chiseled facial features with her finger. "Right now I have only one thing on my mind."

"I see," he said, kissing her neck. "Shall we make ourselves more comfortable?"

Later, they lay side by side in Casey's queen-sized bed. Greg gently caressed her arm, then propped his head on his hand and gazed down at her. "You could make a fortune if you ever decided to sell it."

Casey abruptly sat up. "What was that supposed to mean?" Her voice was sharp. The intimate time they had just shared was shattered.

He kissed her shoulder. "I'm sorry. It was supposed to be a compliment. It was in bad taste."

"Yes, it was," she agreed in an icy tone.

He sighed. "What's wrong, baby? I said I was sorry." He peered at her.

"Don't call me 'baby'," she snapped as she recalled how Josh Barnes frequently used the term.

He stroked her hair. "Okay, what's wrong? What have I done?"

"You haven't done anything, Greg. It's the case I'm working on." She took a deep breath. "Greg, how do you feel about our relationship?"

163

"Casey, I hope you're not asking me to make a commitment to you," he said uneasily as he reached for the pack of cigarettes on the nightstand. He lit one.

"Of course not," she answered. "I'm going to ask you something and I want your honest opinion."

He shrugged his shoulders as he inhaled his cigarette. He slowly exhaled. "Sure."

"How would you say that our relationship is different from say that of a prostitute — I mean besides the obvious monetary gain of a prostitute?"

He frowned. "We choose whom we want to have sex with. I choose you and you choose me. It's not with a total stranger."

"That could be half right."

"Only half right?" He frowned again.

She lay back on her pillow, staring thoughtfully up at the ceiling. "You and I aren't in love with each other. We see each other with only one ultimate goal in mind."

"Okay, so we enjoy being intimate with each other. What's wrong with that? Moreover, I do care very deeply about you, Casey. If I didn't have very strong feelings for you, I certainly wouldn't be here now. I'm not the type who can be intimate with a stranger. You do know that about me."

"I know, and I'm the same way." She ran her fingertips over his cheek, and then closed her eyes. "I don't understand myself anymore." She yawned and then lazily stretched. "I'd better get some sleep. Tomorrow is going to be a hectic day."

"I'd better leave."

"You're not sleeping over?" she asked surprised. "I was going to fix you a wonderful breakfast in the morning."

"As tempting as that sounds, I can't tonight. I've got a brief to finish." He tenderly kissed her lips and then climbed out of bed. Moments later Casey heard the shower. She rolled over onto her side and minutes later was sound asleep.

****

Casey hummed as she walked toward her desk. She hung her raincoat on the coat rack. "Blaine's just fine. She should be out of the hospital in a few days," she excitedly announced.

Jane smiled weakly. "That's good news, Casey." She motioned toward Casey's desk. "Look at the memo on your desk."

"What's going on?" Casey asked as she shuffled through the papers on her cluttered desk. She found the memo and read it. Her mouth dropped open as she clutched the paper in her hand. "What the hell is this?" She glared at Jane. "Some friend you've proven to be!" She sat down at her desk, staring in disbelief at the memo. "I've been reassigned to another case."

"Casey, you've got to understand that it's for your own good." She got up, walked over to her friend, and put her hand on her shoulder. "I don't care if you believe me or not, but I care about you and would never do anything to intentionally hurt you," she said. "It's not healthy for you to stay on this case, especially after what you told me," she reasoned.

"Who's taking my place?" she demanded.

"Lt. Richardson said he'd put the transfer on it."

"Terrific! The transfer." She looked coldly at her partner. "Tonight we were going to bust Barnes. How do you think Kami is going to feel? That kid is laying her life on the line, not to speak of her humiliation! How do you think she's going to feel with a guy taking my place?" She looked disgustedly at Jane. "I can't believe you would deliberately hurt me like this! If this is friendship, I'd rather be alone!"

"I don't know what to say, Casey, to convince you that I

only did this for your own good." She rubbed her chin. "We could go talk to Kami," she said. "She would understand."

"Talk to her! She's going to think I'm backing out on her! She trusted me! I wouldn't expect her to understand." She slammed her fist on the desk. "You really blew it this time, Jane!" Her lips trembled. "You didn't even ask to be put in my place, did you?"

She shook her head. "I thought if I did, it would only further upset you. It'll work out, Casey. Barnes will still get busted tonight. His whole organization is coming down." She walked back over to her own desk and sat down, absentmindedly picking a piece of lint from her skirt. "By the way, where were you last night? All I got was that machine of yours as usual." She smiled. "Did you have a date?"

Casey almost choked. "How can you act so nonchalantly? Personally, it's none of your business where I was last night, so don't try to make small talk with me after you've just shoved a knife in my back!"

"Come on, Casey, you know that's not true. We've got a new case—"

Casey was stunned. "I don't think you understand. I wasn't kidding when I said that we were through as partners. I knew you called last night. I wasn't in the mood to talk to you. In the future please refrain from calling me on my time off unless it concerns a case." Her lips were tightly drawn. She pushed her chair back and rose.

Her words cut straight to Jane's heart. "Where are you going, Casey?"

"First, I'm going to talk to Lt. Richardson, then I'm going home. I've got to think things through." She shook with rage as she grabbed her raincoat. "We're not ready to make our move on Barnes."

"We are. Every one of his apartment buildings and apartments will be raided. We're also going after every person on the list Kami gave us."

"I still don't think we're ready."

"Let me come with you. We've got to talk," Jane pleaded. She had never seen Casey so angry before, and it frightened her. She didn't want their friendship to end this way. She wouldn't allow it to end this way. Casey's stress over Blaine was causing her to think irrationally.

"No! Stay the hell away from me!" she warned as she stormed to Lt. Richardson's office.

Lt. Richardson rubbed his forehead thoughtfully. "I'm sorry, Casey. There's nothing more to say. You and Jane are officially off the case."

"That's not right! I'm this close to busting Barnes!" she screamed.

Lt. Richardson's face reddened in anger. "Watch who you're talking to, Detective!"

Casey threw herself into a chair. "I'm sorry, sir. I just think that you should have talked to me personally before removing me from my case. I've spent a lot of time on it." She wrung her hands. "It's my case," she said firmly.

He leaned back in his chair. "I don't know what your problem is, Jorgan, but I'm giving you a few more days off to pull yourself together."

"I'm fine! I don't need any time off!"

"You get yourself together!" he ordered. "Don't come back until you've resolved whatever it is that's been eating away at you." He cocked an eyebrow. "Don't act so surprised. Don't you think everyone around here has noticed something's changed about you? Get some rest. Now that's an order!"

"I'd like to request a new partner. I can't work with Jane

anymore."

He raised his eyebrows. "You two have worked together for years and have one of the best records in the precinct." He looked suspiciously at her. "So what's happened?"

"I can't work with someone I don't respect or trust any longer."

He laughed loudly. "Get out of here, Jorgan. You're wasting my time." He pointed a finger at her. "Remember, I don't want to see your face around here until you resolve your personal problems."

"Yes, sir," she mumbled.

****

Jane knew by the look on Casey's face that things hadn't gone her way. She felt sorry for her. She looked so tired and pale. She knew if something didn't happen soon Casey was on the verge of a nervous breakdown. She feared for her friend's sanity.

Casey tossed a few items from her desk into her purse.

"Where are you going?" Jane asked.

She blinked back tears. "Thanks to you, I've been given a vacation. Richardson's orders." She threw her bag over her shoulder.

"Casey, I'm sorry."

"Save it!" She turned her back and walked away from Jane.

Jane helplessly watched as Casey disappeared from sight. She knew Casey well enough to know that she would have another agenda. Casey was a fighter and she never gave up easily. Jane sensed that the fight was just beginning.

Chapter Thirteen

Casey paced back and forth across her living room floor. Her mind was in turmoil, and everything was closing in on her. She thought about Blaine and Kami. Kami had been a tough nut to crack, but she had let her defenses down. She had given her trust to Casey. *My word has to count for something, even if nothing else does*, Casey thought. She didn't want to let Kami down the way Jane had let her down. She picked her gun up from the coffee table and jammed it into her belt, then walked out of her apartment, got into her car, and sped over to Kami's.

"Do you know what's coming down tonight?" Casey asked the doorman.

He was uneasy. "Yes…I always knew what was going on, but I was well paid to mind my own business. You can understand my position." He shamefully cast his eyes down toward the floor. "There were always unspoken threats that were added to my paycheck each week." He mopped his forehead with a white handkerchief.

"Yes, I can understand your position," she answered. "You have your job to do and I have mine. Is anyone with Miss Matthews right now?"

"Just the detective that has been assigned to her, Detective

169

Jorgan."

"Okay, that's good. Listen. You understand our plan. Don't say anything or appear nervous," she cautioned. "There will be plenty of backups."

He nodded. "I understand. If you're going up, you'd better hurry. Mr. Barnes will be here shortly."

Casey stepped into the elevator and quickly composed herself on the way to the apartment. Her heart beat so furiously that she could hear it pounding in her ears. She knocked loudly on the apartment door and waited impatiently for Kami's answer.

Cautiously Kami opened the door. "Oh, it's you," she said in a low voice.

Casey heard the distress in her voice. "Can I come in?"

"What for?" Kami's voice was now cool. "You set me up, then walked away. I don't think I can or want to go through with it now." Her hand trembled on the doorknob. "You said I could trust you and I did."

"Kami, I didn't walk out on you. That's why I'm here. I don't have time to explain now, so please just let me in, and I'll explain it all when this is over," she said. "There's no time to lose!" she whispered. "Barnes will be here any minute."

Kami was silent for a moment and then swung the door open. "Okay, I guess you can come in."

"Where's Detective Jackson?"

"Right here, Detective Jorgan," Barry Jackson answered as he walked to the entrance hall. "I understand that you're off this case," he said smugly. "I'd better radio in that you're here."

"Don't you dare!" Casey warned him. "This is my case, Jackson, and don't you forget it!" she stated firmly.

He stood rigidly in front of her. "I've got my orders. Lt.

Richardson said you were pulled off the case for personal reasons."

"Look, Jackson, we don't have much time! You get in another room now! I'm taking over!" she yelled as she pushed past him. "Kami, what time is Barnes expected?" she asked, turning to the puzzled young woman.

"In ten minutes."

Detective Jackson grabbed Casey's arm. "Maybe you didn't understand your orders, Detective! I'm on, you're off!"

Casey smiled mockingly at his boyish-looking face accented by a shock of curly brown hair. "You're just the new kid on the block, Jackson. There's no time to argue about this. Just stay low. I'll take over from here."

"No, you won't!"

"Listen, you idiot! If this gets blown, two young women may very well lose their lives! You want that on your conscience? Now do as I say!" She shoved him toward a hallway. "Stay hidden and don't come out until I give you the all clear signal."

He angrily stomped down the hall.

Casey radioed the officers who were stationed inconspicuously on the busy street below.

****

Kami's palms sweated and her heart beat wildly as she waited for Barnes' arrival. She heard bits and pieces of Casey's conversation. She wondered why Casey wasn't supposed to be on the case anymore, but she was relieved that she was here after all. Casey made her feel safe. When this was over, she wanted to talk to her about something she had been mulling over for days now. She glanced again at Casey, who was wearing a black blazer over a red silk blouse. She was pretty. She noticed that Casey's hair color was almost the same as

171

Blaine's. She'd always loved auburn-colored hair and when she was a child, instead of being grateful for her blonde locks, had instead wished for a different hair color herself. Her mind was whirling with all kinds of strange thoughts and bits and pieces of trivia. She knew, though, it was her mind's way of safeguarding her from dwelling on what was coming down tonight.

Casey caught her eye and winked. She walked over to Kami and firmly placed her hands on the young woman's shoulders as her eyes penetrated Kami's. "Barnes is on his way up." Kami shivered. Casey smiled reassuringly. "We can do this, kid. You and me. Tonight it is finally going to be over. You'll never have to go through this again. We'll get through this together, okay?"

"Yes," Kami whispered. "For Blaine's sake we'll get through this."

"Do you know if Barnes carries a gun?"

"I...I don't know," she stammered. Then the realization of the question struck her. "My God! We might all be killed!"

"No, we won't. I promise you," she whispered.

The familiar knock sounded on the door.

Kami jumped. "I can't do it," she quivered. "It's too dangerous. I'm going to be sick!"

"Calm down," Casey whispered. "Take a deep breath and pull yourself together," she ordered. "We have to do it tonight! Do you understand?"

"I'll try," Kami said hoarsely. "I don't want anything to happen to you."

Casey looked into Kami's frightened eyes. "I'll be fine. Trust me." She squeezed Kami's hand. "It's a piece of cake. Now answer the door before he gets suspicious," she said softly as she tiptoed down the hall.

Kami slowly let her breath out and then flung the door open. "Sorry I took so long. I was in the bathroom," she lied.

"Hi, baby. You're looking as beautiful as ever," Josh said as he planted a kiss on her cheek. "I'd like you to meet Douglas Black."

"How do you do, Mr. Black?"

Douglas smiled appreciatively. "You sure know how to pick them, Barnes."

Kami led the men to the living room, and then proceeded to mix drinks. She took her time preparing the drinks. Douglas Black was tall, thin, and had a receding hairline and ears too big for his head. She guessed him to be in his early sixties.

"Hurry up with the drinks. Mr. Black doesn't have all night."

"Here," Kami said handing Josh a drink. "Here you are, Mr. Black."

"Call me Douglas," he said as he squeezed her thigh. He gulped his drink as he smiled at her.

She stared coolly at him.

"Lighten up, Kami," Josh warned. "Now show Mr. Black to your room."

"But he hasn't finished his drink," she protested.

"Do as you're told," he commanded, then looked apologetically at Black.

****

Casey chewed her bottom lip. She couldn't bear to hear the sounds coming from Kami's bedroom. She heard Black order Kami to lick his entire body. Casey gagged. She received some comfort from the knowledge that this would be the last time Kami would be forced to turn a trick. Kami was pleading with the man to leave her alone, but he persisted. Beads of perspiration broke out on her forehead. She could

173

only imagine what the pervert had Kami doing now and from the sounds coming from the tape, it was as perverted as the first night Casey had listened. She prayed this night to end soon. She wanted Barnes put away for good. She licked her lips in anticipation as she felt her gun in her hand. After what seemed like an eternity, she heard Kami's bedroom door open. She waited for her cue.

"She's some girl, Barnes. Worth every cent," Douglas Black said as he reached into his pocket for his wallet.

"That's why I stay close by when she's working. I can't let anything happen to my best performer." He patted Kami's back then slid his hand further down and gently squeezed her buttocks.

Kami tensed. At any moment, it would be over. Casey would come bursting into the room. She nervously glanced toward the hallway.

"What's the matter with you?" Josh firmly asked. "Don't worry. You'll get your cut." He smiled at Black. "It's always about the money," he chuckled.

Casey stormed into the room, taking all of them by surprise. "Freeze! Get your hands up! You're under arrest!" she shouted as she stood feet slightly apart, her gun pointed at the two men.

Detective Jackson was immediately at her side with his gun drawn.

Douglas Black trembled as sweat broke out on his brow. "I've got a wife...kids...a reputation in this city," he stuttered. "You know who I am, Detective."

"You should have thought about that, Judge!" Casey snapped. "I heard you in the bedroom and it didn't sound like you were thinking about your family then." She tilted her head toward Jackson. "Cuff them and read them their rights."

"I'll pay you...both of you...name your price." His breathing was shallow and sweat ran down the side of his face. "Anything you want, you've got it."

"Are you trying to bribe me?" Casey asked. "Shall I add that to the charges?"

"No...I just thought..." he stammered.

"Well, don't think!"

"You bitch!" Josh Barnes spat as he lunged at Kami, catching her around the neck. He dragged her in front of himself. He looked at Casey and Jackson. "You going to shoot her? To get to me you're going to have to go through her."

Kami's frightened eyes pierced Casey's heart. "Let her go, Barnes," she ordered. "You'll never get away."

"No way! She's going to get me out of here!" He backed toward the entrance hall. "No one's going to do anything to me and risk hurting her. I'm not that stupid."

"I'll cover him," Jackson said.

"No, I want him," Casey insisted. "You won't get far, Barnes. The police are on their way up now. They heard everything that's been going on here tonight. The place is wired."

Josh laughed. "If they can get in. I figured my pretty little girl was up to something," he said as he tightened his grip on Kami's throat. "So I locked the lobby door. As for John, let's just say that he's indisposed and won't be opening the door for anyone tonight. At least the door will slow them down."

Casey walked toward him.

"Come any closer and her neck will snap like a pencil." He kept backing toward the door. "She's my insurance policy." He smiled at Casey. "You know, I never could stand a bossy woman, especially one who's a cop!" he snarled as he slowly brought his other hand up, revealing his gun. Then he menacingly aimed it at Casey. "It wouldn't bother me in the least to spill some of your blood, lady cop!"

"Josh, no!" Kami cried.

"Shut up! I'll take care of you later!"

"I can get him," Jackson whispered.

"No, it's too risky. Backups should be here any second."

"Hey, cop, you're not so bad-looking yourself. I could make some big bucks with you! Maybe get you to wear a cute little policewoman outfit. The guys would really go for that." Barnes sneered. "Of course, I like to try out the merchandise myself before offering it to the public to make sure it's top quality."

"In your dreams, scumbag," Casey snarled.

Douglas Black shakily tried to grab Casey's arm. She shoved him aside and Jackson forced him to the floor where he pissed his pants.

"I don't like being called names," Josh said angrily. "Don't press your luck with me."

"Truth hurt, Barnes?" Casey asked.

"Open up! Police!"

"What now, lady cop?" Josh laughed.

"Stand down!" Casey yelled. "He's got the girl and he's armed!"

Josh pointed the gun at Kami's head. "All I have to do is pull the trigger." He grinned. "You're not going to shoot me and risk Kami's life. Now are you?"

"Try me," Casey answered.

Tears streamed down Kami's face. "Please, Josh, just go. I won't press any charges. You can leave the country!"

"Don't make me laugh, baby." He tightened his hold on her. "After I spill this bitch's blood, you're next, Kami." He eyed Casey. "Anything else you want to say, bitch?"

Casey smiled. "You're bluffing. There's nowhere to run, Barnes, so you might as well give up now." She sighed impatiently. "Now toss your gun over here." She kept her eyes fixed on him as he aimed the gun at her. "Put it down, Barnes," she warned as she watched the tears spilling down Kami's pale cheeks. She looked into Josh's flaming eyes. She never blinked as he pulled the trigger.

Chapter Fourteen

Kami screamed. She turned, brought her knee up, and caught Josh in the groin. He still held tightly to his gun, but his arm slipped from Kami as he doubled over. Kami hysterically ran behind Detective Jackson.

"Freeze! Throw the gun down!" Jackson ordered.

Josh painfully tried to straighten up as he pointed his gun at Jackson. "You're a dead man," he panted.

Jackson fired a shot. He watched as Barnes grabbed his chest and slumped to the floor at the same time the police burst into the room.

Kami ran to Casey kneeling over her. She was sobbing uncontrollably when Jane reached her. "My God, Casey!" Jane screamed. "We need an ambulance!"

"An ambulance is on the way," Jackson said as he laid a hand on Jane's shoulder. "She's a brave woman, a lot braver than I would have been. She stood up to Barnes. She thought he was bluffing."

"You can fill me in on the details later, Jackson. She's bleeding badly. Kami, get me some fresh towels." Jane unbuttoned Casey's blouse as Jackson helplessly stood by. "It's bad, Jackson. Where's the ambulance?"

"They're here," Jackson answered as the paramedics

surrounded Casey.

Kami came back with the towels. "How is she?" she asked in a trembling voice.

"Not good. Her vital signs are weak," Jane said.

"We've got to get her to the hospital and quick!" one of the paramedics ordered.

Lt. Richardson rushed over to the two detectives. "Barnes is dead and Black is on his way to the station. We'll need a full report from you, Jackson." He shook his head. "What the hell was Jorgan doing here?"

"I don't know, Lieutenant. I told her to leave, but it was too late. Barnes was already on his way up," Jackson answered. "She insisted it was her case."

"We'll straighten it all out later." He shook his head again. "She's a damned good cop—stubborn, but one of the best. Nothing better happen—" He didn't finish his sentence, but stood silently watching as the medics did their work.

Kami watched as Casey was loaded on a stretcher with tubes and bottles sticking out from everywhere it seemed. Bright red blood slowly sank into the fibers of the white carpet. Josh's words came back to haunt her. He had promised to spill Casey's blood and he had kept his word. "She's got to make it," she prayed.

Jackson stood next to Jane. "I know there's been problems between you and Detective Jorgan," he said as he shuffled his feet uncomfortably.

Jane faced him, looking at him sharply. "Casey and I do not see eye to eye on everything, and I'm certainly not concerned with idle precinct gossip," she stated.

"I'm sorry."

"Did Casey kill Barnes?"

Jackson stared directly at her. "No, I did."

"I'm grateful that you were here, Jackson," she said in a softer tone of voice. "You saved Kami's life. And Casey's," she added. She looked over at Kami who sat huddled on the floor with her arms wrapped around her legs. She was shaking so hard Jane thought she was going to convulse. Jane knelt beside her.

"Is she going to...?" Kami asked.

"Don't even think that," she said in a shaky voice. "Casey's tough. She's a fighter. In no time at all, she's going to be back on her feet." She patted Kami's hand. "We owe a lot to you for helping us on this case, Kami. If it weren't for you, we never would have gotten Barnes."

"She was so brave. She stood right up to him. I never saw anyone do that to him before."

Jane smiled. "That's Casey. If there's a better cop in this city than her, I'd like to know who it is."

"They're getting ready to take her to the ambulance," Barry Jackson said as he stood towering above the women. "I'll stay with Miss Matthews if you'd like to ride in the ambulance with her, Detective Adams," he offered.

Jane stood up. "Thank you, Jackson. I appreciate it. Don't worry, Kami, everything will be okay. I'll let you know the minute I hear anything."

****

Jane held Casey's hand on the ride to the hospital. "How serious is it?" Her voice quivered as she questioned the paramedic who was busily monitoring Casey's vital signs.

The man frowned. "It's hard to say at this point. She's lost a lot of blood." He cleared his throat. "We don't know if the bullet penetrated any vital organs. All I can tell you is that we'll have to wait and see what the ER doctors say."

Jane forced herself to hold back tears as she looked

180

at her partner's unconscious form. Casey couldn't die, she thought. She had too much to live for. Blaine wasn't even aware that she had a sister. Jane suddenly realized how unfair she'd been to her. Casey had to live; she needed to tell her how wrong she'd been. She should have celebrated Casey's finding Blaine. Casey had only confided the information to her because she'd hounded her so. Jane squeezed Casey's hand. "You're going to make it," she whispered.

"Damn," the paramedic muttered. "We're losing her."

****

Kami rushed into the waiting room. "Did you hear anything yet?" she asked.

Jane rubbed her aching eyes. "No, nothing yet." She stretched. "You shouldn't have come here, Kami. After everything you've been through tonight, you should be home resting."

Kami took a seat next to her. "I...I couldn't. I had to come. Detective Jorgan saved my life tonight." Her eyes misted.

Jane squeezed Kami's shoulder. She understood the depth of the woman's emotions because she felt the same way.

They waited for hours. Officers from the precinct came and went. Lt. Richardson had sat for a couple of hours and then was called back to the station. He gave strict orders to Jane to call him the minute she had any news on Casey's condition. Every once in a while Jane tried to make small talk with Kami, but then lapsed into silence, each too wrapped up in her own thoughts and fears to be of much comfort to one another.

Finally, the waiting room door opened, and a surgeon walked toward them.

They both jumped to their feet. Jane's heart pounded as she looked questioningly at his somber expression. Her throat dried out and she could barely speak. "What is it, Doctor?" she choked. "How is she?"

Dr. Reynolds ran his hand through his graying hair. "Does Detective Jorgan have any immediate family?"

"Oh, my God!" Jane cried. "No…what's wrong?"

He cleared his throat.

Kami shook so violently that she had to grip the back of a chair for support.

"We have a problem. Unless we can get an immediate transfusion, we're going to lose her. There's nothing more we can do at this point," he said quietly. "She's lost too much blood and we're trying to stop it."

"I'll do it," Jane immediately offered.

"I wish it were that easy," he said. "She has a rare blood type and I don't know if you'll be a compatible donor, but we'll have you tested."

"Can't you get the blood from some other facility or hospital?" Kami asked.

"We're working on it, but it doesn't look promising. She's had several transfusions already and we've just about exhausted our supply. We have some being flown in, but time is of the essence here."

"If she gets the transfusion, will she be all right?" Jane asked.

"If we can get the bullet out. It's just below her heart. She was very lucky."

"Why can't you remove it?" Jane asked.

"I need to know that there will be enough blood available. Removing the bullet from this particular area is extremely critical." He patted her hand reassuringly. "Please, let's waste no more time."

"I'd like to be tested also," Kami said in a small voice.

Jane hugged the younger woman. "Thank you," she whispered. "I'm going to call the precinct and get as many officers down here as I can."

Jane and Kami paced back and forth in the waiting room, anxiously awaiting Dr. Reynolds' report on the compatibility of the donors' blood to Casey's. Moments later he entered the room.

From the expression on his face, Jane knew that neither she nor Kami had matched.

"I'm sorry," he said in a quiet voice. "But we do have a lot of volunteers to test, thanks to your precinct. They're all being tested as we speak. I hope that we'll come up with someone out of the group. I could go ahead and proceed, but I'm afraid that she'll need a little more blood than we have available. I have to make a decision in the next few minutes." He turned to leave when Jane grabbed his arm.

"Casey does have a sister, but the woman doesn't know that Casey is her sister," she blurted out.

Dr. Reynolds skeptically raised his eyebrows.

"It's a long story, Doctor, but if I can get her to do this—"

"Her blood has to match," he interrupted her.

"Yes, I know. If it does, would you have time?" Her eyes pleaded with his.

"Time isn't on our side," he said slowly. "Let's hope we can keep her stabilized. Try to hurry."

"I'll go talk to her sister," Jane shouted over her shoulder as she dragged a bewildered Kami out of the room.

As the elevator stopped at Blaine's floor, Kami suddenly realized what was going on. "It's Blaine!" she exclaimed.

"That's why Casey acted so weird."

"Yes," Jane answered as they hurried down the corridor. "I'll explain it all to you later."

"You don't have to. Now I know why Detective Jorgan asked me so many questions about Blaine's past."

Blaine woke up alarmed when Jane and Kami barged into her room. "What's wrong? Where's Detective Jorgan? She promised to keep me posted about Josh. Wasn't everything supposed to come down last night?" Her eyes darted from one to the other. "Something went wrong, didn't it? That's why you're here in the middle of the night!"

Jane tried to compose herself. "Blaine, we need your help. Casey's surprise will be ruined, but it can't be helped. You're the only one who may be able to save her life!" Jane rambled.

Blaine propped herself up as she looked from Jane to Kami. "What are you talking about? What's happened to Detective Jorgan?"

"She's been shot," Kami said bluntly.

"No!" Blaine covered her mouth with her hand. "Did Josh do it?" she moaned.

"Yes, Blaine. He's dead. It's over," Kami answered. "But before he was killed, he shot Detective Jorgan. She desperately needs blood. If she doesn't get it soon, she'll die."

Blaine's mind was whirling. "I don't understand, Kami. How can I help? You two aren't making any sense. Why don't they just give her the blood she needs?"

Jane swallowed hard. "Just listen to what I have to say, Blaine. Don't say anything, just listen, please! There's not much time."

"Okay," she agreed, looking quizzically at Kami.

"Here it is in a nutshell. You are Casey's baby sister. If your blood is compatible, which it hopefully is, then you can save Casey's life."

Blaine didn't say anything for a full minute. Jane's confession stunned her. Was she dreaming or was Jane really telling her that Casey Jorgan was her older sister? She wasn't sure how to react to the news. Part of her had longed for the day she would find out that she did have a biological brother or sister, but another part of her was frightened. She inhaled deeply. "I…I can't believe it," she whispered. "How long have you known, Kami?"

"I just found out," Kami answered. "I know it's a shock, Blaine, but finding your roots is all you've ever wanted."

"I've known for only a short time myself. I forced it out of her," Jane admitted. "That's why the situation between us has been tense. She had planned in detail how she was going to tell you, Blaine. She hasn't known long herself. When we were handed your case, it ripped her apart knowing what you were going through." Her bottom lip trembled as she gripped Blaine's hands. "Please help her," she choked. "She'll die if you don't. Time's running out for her!"

Blaine blinked back tears. "Yes, I will. I have to!"

****

Casey's eyes fluttered briefly then opened. She squinted, giving them time to adjust to the bright sunlight streaming through the window.

"Casey, welcome back!" Jane exclaimed. A smile broke across her face. "I don't like being a loner. Before you know it, we'll be hitting the streets together again, partner."

"I think we'll have to…discuss that later, Jane," she said.

Kami squeezed Casey's hand. "You sure had me scared." She swallowed hard. "Thank you, Detective Jorgan, for giving me a new life." She looked down at Casey's pale face. "As soon as you get out of here, I'd like to have a long talk with

185

you."

Casey smiled weakly. "Sure, kid," she whispered.

Blaine stood on the other side of Casey's bed staring down at her, but she said nothing.

"What's wrong, Blaine?" Casey asked as she sipped at a glass of water. "Blaine, it's over now." She smiled. "It's so good to see you on your feet again."

Blaine blinked back tears as she pushed her hair from her brow. "I...I gave some blood for you," she said.

"Thank you, Blaine. That was very kind of you."

"Casey...I—" Blaine began.

Casey smiled. "Hey, kid," she interrupted. "Do you realize that this is the first time you've called me by my name instead of detective?"

Tears poured down Blaine's face.

Casey looked at Kami and Jane, but could read nothing in their faces.

"I know we're sisters," Blaine sobbed as she threw her arms around Casey's neck.

Casey tried to swallow the lump, which had formed in her throat, as she too began to cry. "Blaine, I'm sorry I didn't tell you. I had it all planned—"

"It doesn't matter," Blaine broke in. "All that matters is that you're going to be all right and that we've finally found each other. We have so much to talk about."

Jane grabbed Kami's arm. "Come on, let's leave them alone for a while. They have a lot of catching up to do." She dabbed at her eyes as she left the room.

****

Barry Jackson hesitated outside of Casey's hospital room. He straightened his tie and then threw his shoulders back as he walked into the room. Casey was sleeping, so he tiptoed to the chair by the side of her bed and sat down. He nervously clutched the bouquet of flowers he held in his sweaty hand as he gazed at the peaceful expression on her face. She was so beautiful, he thought. Lying like she was now, so vulnerable, it was hard to imagine how tough she really was.

Casey yawned, then stretched. She turned, alarmed when she spotted him. "How long have you been here, Jackson?" she asked sharply.

"Just a few minutes." His face reddened. "I'm sorry if I've disturbed you," he said. "I brought these for you." He thrust the flowers at her.

Casey's eyes softened. "Thank you, Jackson. They're beautiful. Could you please put them in the vase over there?" She pointed to the windowsill.

"Sure." He smiled. After he put the flowers in the vase, he walked over to her bed.

"Yes, Jackson?" She felt uncomfortable with him standing so close.

"Do you think you could call me Barry?" he asked. "This Jackson business is getting to me."

Casey burst into laughter. "I'm sorry. I didn't mean to offend you. I've spent too many years in the precinct."

"I accept your apology, but I really do think that you meant to offend me." He returned her laughter.

"Okay, I admit it." She took a long look at him. "Please call me Casey," she said.

His eyes grew warm. "I heard around the precinct that you're not seeing anyone…seriously." He smiled awkwardly, wishing he had rephrased his remark. He was embarrassed that Casey made him feel like a bumbling teenager.

She smiled coyly. "Why, Jackson…sorry, Barry, are you trying to ask me out?"

"Well, it didn't come out the way I planned, but yes, I'd like to take you out for a night on the town just as soon as they spring you from here."

"How can I possibly refuse you?" She smiled again. "You saved my life."

"You're some woman, Casey. You've got more guts than all the guys in the precinct put together."

"I think you're exaggerating just a little. I do have my moments, though." She winked. "If you're lucky, I'll tell you about my escapades someday."

"That'll be my lucky day."

Chapter Fifteen

Blaine inhaled the clean, fresh air. She gazed at the twinkling lights of the city below. "I feel like I'm dreaming," she murmured. "Who would have ever dreamed that we've lived all these years in Philadelphia and never knew one another. It makes me wonder if we ever were in the same movie theater or restaurant at the same time. Do you know what I mean?"

Casey laid a hand on her shoulder. "I know exactly what you mean." She sighed. "You'll never know how hard it was for me to see you after you were attacked. I wanted so desperately to tell you that you weren't alone—that you had someone who cared about you and shared your life."

Blaine turned and faced her sister. "I never dreamed you'd be so beautiful."

Casey blushed. "It must run in the family, then. Did I ever tell you that you're the image of our mother?"

"Really? Is that where I get my yen for Italian food?"

Casey laughed. "It sure is. There's so much I want to share with you. You took after our mother and I resemble our father."

"I want to know everything you remember about them."

"You will. We're family. It feels so good to say that. I have

189

a family." Her eyes filled with tears. "I couldn't be happier, Blaine. My life has so much meaning and purpose now. I feel whole. I knew I had a baby sister somewhere because you'd been a part of my life for six months, but no one would ever tell me what had happened to you."

"I'm so glad you found me." She was thoughtful for a moment. "I hope you won't be angry with me, Casey, but Kami and Jane are coming over tonight. Kami and I want to talk to you two about something."

"What?"

"I'll wait until they get here." She sat down. "There is one little thing that bothers me, though."

Casey raised her eyebrows. "What is it, Blaine?"

She ran her hand through her thick hair. "It's you and Jane. I feel responsible for what's happened to your friendship." She gazed at her sister. "After all, you've got to remember that if Jane hadn't known about me, you may not have gotten the blood you needed and may have died. Then I never would have known I had a sister."

Casey walked over to Blaine and put an arm around her shoulder. "I've thought about that too. I know I've been unfair to Jane and I have no excuse for my behavior. It's my stubbornness. That also comes from Mom."

Blaine laughed.

"But you know what?"

"What?"

"Tonight I intend to remedy that. I miss her. Everything's been happening so fast. But I do need to talk to her and ask her forgiveness for the way I've been treating her lately."

Blaine smiled as she threw her arms around Casey's neck. "I also want to thank you for letting me stay here."

"Where else do you think I'd have my baby sister stay?

Besides, it's great having you here. I never realized how much I do hate living alone."

"Do you think we'll ever catch up on each other's lives?" Blaine asked.

Casey was thoughtful. "I don't know, but it doesn't really matter. Who cares about the past? We've got a terrific future. That's all that really matters."

Blaine grinned when she heard the doorbell. "That must be Kami and Jane," she called over her shoulder as she rushed to the door.

"Blaine, you look great!" Kami exclaimed, embracing her friend.

Jane stood silently in the foyer.

"Come on in, you two," Blaine said as she led them into the living room. "Kami, would you help me prepare some snacks in the kitchen?"

"I'd love to!"

"Do you mind if I sit down?" Jane asked.

"Of course not," Casey replied.

Jane seated herself on the sofa and folded her hands in her lap. She looked at Casey, who was leaning against the mantle with an amused expression on her face.

"Nice weather we're having," Jane announced, breaking the silence.

Casey burst into laughter as she walked across the room and threw her arms around Jane. "Nice weather?" she giggled. "Is that all you can think of to say to your best friend?"

Jane started to laugh too. "What do you expect me to say?" she choked. "You haven't spoken to me in weeks."

Casey sat next to her and took her hand. Her expression became serious. "I know I've been a bitch. I won't make excuses for my behavior, but for so long the only purpose in my life was finding my baby sister. I almost went crazy when I found out that she was alive, well, and living here in the city. All I could think about was reuniting with her. I had only learned the truth shortly before we were handed Blaine's case." She frowned. "I had this fantasy about how I was going to tell her. I never imagined it would be any other way."

"And I blew it for you. Right?"

"You kept nagging me about the case. I didn't want anyone to know. I wanted to make everyone pay for what Blaine was going through. Unfortunately, you received the brunt of my anger." She let her breath out slowly. "I had no right to take out my feelings on you. You were right to tell Blaine the truth. You were put in a tight squeeze. I realize that now. You were very instrumental in saving my life, and I want to thank you for that. And I want to thank you for being there when I needed your strength. I'm sorry for all the hurtful things I said to you."

Jane hugged her. "I've missed you."

"Here we go," Blaine announced as she set a tray of cookies and milk on the coffee table.

Kami followed, setting a tray of glasses down.

Jane raised her eyebrows. "Cookies and milk?"

Blaine feigned surprise. "You mean to tell me that you two have been friends for all these years, Jane, and you didn't know that Casey's favorite nighttime snack is chocolate chip cookies dunked in milk?"

Jane laughed as she picked up a cookie and a glass of milk Kami had poured. "I'll have to try it. I haven't done this since I was a little girl."

Kami and Blaine sat on the floor and leaned their elbows on the coffee table, staring at the two detectives.

"What's it like being a cop?" Kami asked as she dunked

a cookie.

"It's the only career for me," Casey answered as she bit into a soggy cookie. "I wouldn't know how or want to do anything else."

"It's exciting, rewarding, and fulfilling. Never a dull moment," Jane said as she sipped her milk.

"You have to dunk your cookie, Jane," Casey instructed.

Jane picked up a cookie and dipped it into the cold milk then took a bite. "Not bad!"

"Okay, what's with you two?" Casey asked.

Blaine and Kami looked at each other and grinned.

"I think Blaine should have the honor of telling you and Jane," Kami said.

"Tell us what?" Jane asked.

Blaine got to her feet. "We have a very important announcement to make." She hesitated dramatically as she pulled Kami to her feet. "Are you ready for this? It's guaranteed to blow your minds!"

"Enough already! Tell us!" Casey laughed.

"Without further ado, I'd like to announce that Kami and I are leaving Monday morning!"

"Leaving? Why? Blaine, you can't go now!" Casey cried. "We're just getting to know one another."

Blaine ran over to her sister and excitedly grabbed her hand. Her eyes were sparkling. "No, you don't understand. We've been accepted into the police academy!" she squealed. "You go back to work on Monday, so it'll work out perfectly!"

Casey's jaw dropped. "I don't believe it!" She hugged her sister and then Kami.

Jane grinned broadly. "You two are going to make quite a team!" She threw her arms around Blaine and Kami.

"Just like you and Casey," Kami said. "We thought it

over, liked the idea more and more, so we had Lt. Richardson set us up, and made him promise not to tell you two."

"I think I know what made my mind up," Blaine said with a sly grin.

"Oh? And what was that?" Casey asked.

"When this tough-talking female detective kept calling me 'kid'. I loved her attitude!"

Casey laughed.

"One more thing," Blaine said. "Tomorrow night we're all going to belatedly celebrate my sister's big three-oh."

"I've already received the best present I could ever ask for." Casey put her arms around Blaine. "The four of us will make quite a team…kid!"

Susan K. Droney

AUTHOR

Writing is Susan's number one passion. When she isn't writing, she enjoys reading, spending time in her garden, and visiting family and friends. She has many novels, short stories, and magazine articles to her credit. Raised in western New York, she now resides in New Jersey. For information about Susan's current and upcoming titles, please visit http://www.susandroney.com or http://susandroney.blogspot.com